LAVENDER LOVE SONGS
A COLLECTION OF SAPPHIC ROMANCE NOVELLAS

ROCHELLE WOLF

AURORA INKWELL MEDIA

Copyright © 2025 by Rochelle Wolf

Aurora Inkwell Media.

All rights reserved.

eBook ISBN: 978-1-7383392-7-3

Paperback IBSN: 978-1-7383392-6-6

No part of this publication may be reproduced, distributed, or transmitted in any form or by any means, including photocopying, recording, or other electronic or mechanical methods, without the prior written permission of the publisher, except as permitted by Canadian copyright law. For permission requests, contact hello@rochellewolf.com.

The story, all names, characters, and incidents portrayed in this production are fictitious. No identification with actual persons (living or deceased), places, buildings, and products is intended or should be inferred.

Act Two Copyright © 2024 by Rochelle Wolf

Room For Two Copyright © 2024 by Rochelle Wolf

Song For You Copyright © 2025 by Rochelle Wolf

Cover Design by Maria Casacalenda.

Editing by Annie Percik (alobear.co.uk)

No part of this book or cover has been created with AI. No part of this book or cover is permitted for use in training AI.

First edition 2025.

www.rochellewolf.com

BOOKS BY ROCHELLE WOLF

Included in this collection:

Act Two: A sapphic second chance novella

Room for Two: A sapphic friends to lovers forced proximity romance novella

Song For You: A queer romance novella

Other novellas & writing:

Returning for You: A sweet XF holiday romance novella

Contributor to the Amazon best-selling *Heart's Lock, Love's Key: A Valentine's Day Anthology*

Impossible Match: a sapphic arranged marriage romance

(coming summer 2025)

CONTENTS

Introduction — vii

ACT TWO — 1
ROOM FOR TWO — 69
SONG FOR YOU — 145

Bonus Material — 221
Acknowledgments — 223
About the Author — 225

INTRODUCTION

When *Act Two* first came out in June 2024, I knew I wanted to put it in a physical collection one day but was unsure of when that day would be. Less than a year later, I'm so excited to be able to share not just that story, but two other novellas that I have written since then. Each story stands out on its own but I find they also work well when read in order, with each story building on the characters that were found in the stories prior.

Thank you to all the readers who accepted my cozy, warm stories with open hearts and minds. Thank you to those who kept asking when they could buy them in another format.

I hope each story, or love song, keeps you warm. The world needs cozy stories featuring queer joy and love now more than ever, and I hope you enjoy my small contribution to this important mission.

With all my love,

Rochelle

ACT TWO

Sometimes love is worth rewriting—is it time to move their love from the wings and onto center stage?

Gabriella Adams has done her best to forget it all.

It's been a year since her whirlwind situationship with Jenna Daniels—the theater actor that managed to sneak backstage into her heart—ended and she's ready to move on. Gabriella refuses to linger on lost feelings for an old flame and is set on making the most of her newfound singleness…and she's been doing amazing, thank you very much.

But when Jenna shows up unexpectedly hoping to be friends again, it throws Gabriella for a loop. She wasn't expecting an encore on their relationship and as old feelings resurface, Gabriella has to decide whether there was a deeper reason for their split, or if it was distance and the wall she's always had around her heart that drove them apart. Are they ready for their next act to begin?

CHAPTER ONE

I'm pulled away from my nutritious dinner of popcorn in bed by a knock at the door. Which is weird, because when was the last time anyone came over?

I groan as I reluctantly roll out of bed, stopping at the bathroom to rinse my cheese-covered fingertips. Whoever it is can wait a few moments, please and thank you.

I peek through the peephole.

Oh my god, what is Jenna doing here?

My heartbeat quickens as I do my best not to panic. I step back into the bathroom to make sure I look more like the 'hot' in hot mess, rather than the 'mess' I'm sure I'm giving.

My hair is dull but at least it's clean, and my clothes are thankfully stain-free. Thank goodness I'm wearing sweatpants and a baggy *Abbott Elementary* T-shirt.

I open the door.

God, she still looks good.

The spring chill has her bundled up in a puffy down jacket and somehow the pink earmuffs over her blonde hair manage to make her look more put together than I ever could be out in the cold.

She smiles that beautiful smile I've missed so much. I try not to look dumbfounded as she speaks.

"Long time no see," she begins.

"Yes."

"Can I come in? It's four degrees out." She awkwardly giggles as she says it.

I'm in trouble.

"Sure."

I stand back as she walks up the stairs and into the house. As she removes her boots and various accessories, I try very hard not to think about the last time she was here...

Pressed up against the wall. The couch covered in our clothes. The sun warming the bed sheets.

I snap out of it as she stops just inside the door and looks around.

"Still the same," she notes.

"Would you like some water?" I ask. That seems like a safe question.

She nods and we awkwardly make our way to the kitchen where I pour her a glass from the Brita water filter. She heads towards the couch and I use the silence to grab my own glass. Whatever she has to say, I guess I need to hear it.

I join her on the couch, trying not to sit too close to her. I force myself still, aiming for a friendly distance.

"How long are you in town for?" I ask.

"A while, I'm the understudy for the lead role in *Mean Girls.*"

"Ah, for work." It slips out but I don't apologize. Of course, it's for work.

Not that I have unresolved feelings; really, I'm over it.

I don't sound convincing, even to myself.

Jenna smiles. "I've missed you too, Gabby."

My heart melts a bit, as hard as I try to stop it. She was the only one I let call me a nickname and it's bittersweet to hear it now, almost a year later.

I try to smile in a way I hope looks friendly, and *just* friendly.

"Well...it's nice to see you. I'm happy to see you're doing well. Really."

It's the best I can manage right now.

She sighs and stands.

"I should let you get back to your night...I just wanted to see you and invite you to the show sometime. I cover the Thursday evening performances, if you'd like a ticket."

I nod and walk her out, doing my best to keep my distance. I'm afraid I'll cross a line again and I want to keep the past firmly in the past. When she leaves and I've returned to rotting in my bed, I indulge in secretly stalking her public profile, scrolling carefully to make sure no post is liked—whether on her profile or that of any of her friends.

This is going to be a shitshow. And if that yellow bus from the movie production could come and hit me now, I'd welcome it with open arms.

CHAPTER TWO

"Let me get this straight. Your ex is back in town and the first thing she basically did was visit you, at night, to invite you to her new show, and that was it?" Tyler interrogates me while we wait for our food to arrive.

Nights like this are sometimes the only thing that gets me through the week. A nice evening out with your bestie...perfectly timed to take advantage of all the happy hour deals, because regular-priced Toronto restaurants are no joke. This week, we're trying a new Italian place that has unlimited pasta for under $20. We're here to test it out before the TikTok influencers take over and make the wait times unbearable. I can picture the viral video already.

"First of all, not an ex. Second of all, yes, that is what happened."

Tyler takes a deliberate sip of his drink. I can tell he's about to enter 'lecture Gabriella mode'.

"You know I love you and will support you always, but y'all were together, no matter what bullshit Gen Z label you put on it, and I hate to say it, but I think you should go."

Now it's my turn to take a deliberate slow sip. The alcohol stings but I need it tonight.

"I don't think it's a good idea. It took a lot for me to try and forget her..."

"You don't have to go see her in a romantic way. Maybe you can just be friends."

"Maybe," I reply weakly.

Tyler knows how much her departure broke me, how much I wanted her to stay. How hard it was in the beginning.

He reaches out and grabs my hand.

"You're stronger than you even know. I know you've always wanted to see her perform, so maybe this is the time to do it. You can close out the memories with a friendly time."

I sigh and take another sip of my drink. I guess it would be nice to end the situation amicably. I've never liked to leave things unresolved, and this could be the final line of code in the program that was our relationship.

"Are you processing this via a weird computer analogy again?"

"Why do you even ask, if you know the answer?"

We laugh. In true Tyler nature, he begins his toast with a book analogy—his chosen area of interest.

"Well, here's cheers to closing out a weird chapter of your life and starting a new blank page."

"Who's making weird analogies now?" I giggle as our glasses clink.

Tyler winks. "Whatever happens, I'll be here there to pick up the torn pages of your heart."

"I think you're getting your metaphors mixed up, but thank you. No torn pages here."

The walk home is nice, and the spring chill feels bearable as I'm fuelled by the drinks from the restaurant. I make it home in record time and toss my jacket on the front bench.

Jenna threw her own jacket there when she was here yesterday.

I shake my head to clear the thought. I grab myself a glass of water. She did look beautiful, as always.

I've done my best to bury the memories over the past year, but they come bubbling up anyway. The intimate moments, the soft sighs, her very kissable lips, and her silky skin.

"Get a grip, Gabriella," I say aloud to myself.

Maybe Tyler is right, maybe I should just meet up with her so I can close out these feelings and get a fresh start. Go on the apps again. *Ugh*.

I grab my phone and flop onto the couch. Against my better judgment, I still have Jenna's phone number.

> hey, it's Gabriella. not sure if you still have my number

Maybe I shouldn't have included that last bit...is it too mean? I begin scrolling on social media and her reply comes back faster than I anticipated.

> of course i still have it - great to hear from you Gabs

There's that pesky nickname again.

> only you could get away with that

> with what? 😊

> so does your offer still stand? i have to admit i've always wanted to see Mean Girls live

> really? you'll come see it? absolutely you can

> please, i'd love for you to be there

> i have to go to sleep now (early rehearsal day tomorrow) but i'll text you soon with the details

And because I'm powerless to resist...

> sure - sweet dreams

> goodnight darling 🩶

~

U*ghhhh.* I slam my ThinkPad shut.

Thank God I'm home alone so no one else can witness that outburst. Why do computer programs always glitch at exactly 4:59pm and not a minute earlier? It's always as if the universe is conspiring against me.

Not today, Satan. I have important business to do.

But first, I answer a FaceTime call from Tyler. Technically, he started the call in our group chat with Leslie but she's typically wrangling her adorable child at this time of day so her absence from the call is not unusual.

"Hey babes, everything okay?" I say as his face appears on the screen.

I place my phone down on a nearby stand so I can fiddle with the stress ball on my desk. Tyler sits at his own desk, similarly perching a phone against what must be a pen holder because the angle is wonky. His brown hair droops into his face as he looks down at his phone, and he pushes it up every couple of seconds.

"Just had the worst day at work. I mean, technically, I should still be working but it's 5pm and I do not get paid enough for that."

"I feel that." I sigh in sympathy.

"You get paid enough to keep working, though," he chuckles. "Is this a bad time?"

"No, I had to step away. I need to be completely zen today... I'm seeing Jenna's show tonight."

"Wow, why is this the first I'm hearing of it?"

"Sorry, work was so busy! You know how hectic this time of

year gets, with everyone deciding they want everything done yesterday and not a day later."

"Are you going to see her before the show?"

I watch as, on-screen, Tyler moves to sit on his couch. I recognize the bookshelves that appear behind him, a staple in the marketing videos he does for his job at an indie press in the city.

"No, she has to spend the day in warm-ups and preparation. The ticket is waiting at the box office for me."

Tyler hums in understanding. "You'll have to debrief me later but, in the meantime, do you have time to listen to me rant?"

"Of course! I'll do my makeup while we talk."

"Wow, makeup...it's almost as if you expect to see her today, despite no plans being made about it. Is she going to spot you all the way from the stage?"

I laugh and don't respond. His teasing, while annoying, is not exactly inaccurate. Maybe a part of me is hoping to see her.

"Oh, shut up, it's a theatre. A place of prestige! It's not like I can show up as my usual troll goblin self."

"Sure, it's for the arts. Whatever you need to tell yourself."

I don't usually indulge in treats or solo adventures but a slight nervousness about the evening kicks in and I decide to treat myself to sushi at the restaurant across from the theatre before the show. It took less time than anticipated to get ready and finish talking to Tyler, and I have a solid hour until the show starts.

I grab a small table for one and scroll through my phone as I wait for my order to arrive. I'm in the middle of texting a picture of my food to my family group chat (they enjoy updates like this) when a text from Jenna comes in.

> sorry gabs today was so hectic. i hope you enjoy the show - do you want to grab drinks after? i know a cheap happy hour spot that serves $3 tacos

Against my better judgment, I reply right away with a yes. If Tyler were here, he'd definitely tease me about how my backbone could use some extra work but I ignore the imaginary criticism and focus on the fact, or rather, the hope that this will bring about exactly what I need right now. And whether that's closure or not, I have to find out for myself.

CHAPTER THREE

Getting my ticket at the box office turns out to be surprisingly simple and I let the crowd lead me into the theatre. When I get to the usher, they direct me to my seat and I take their printed guide.

The seat is in the small box to the left of the stage and it's comforting to be sitting amongst only a handful of people, compared to the usual crowds below in the main area of the theatre. I politely smile at the person seated next to me (perhaps another actor's family member?) and flip through the guide.

As with most shows that feature understudies instead of the main cast, a white slip of paper informs me of the substitutions and a hint of pride flushes through me when I read "Jenna Daniels as Cady Heron" on the page. The back of the paper has her acting bio.

Jenna Daniels made her acting debut right here in Toronto in various productions, including Hamlet, Monty Python's Spamalot, and Frankenstein Revived at the Stratford Festival. Her acts have taken her across the world, including a year stint on the infamous Disney Cruise Line. Mean Girls Live is her Mirvish debut.

I take a deep breath and put my phone on silent. I glance around the theatre, noting the families and couples and other solo attendees like me. Despite everything, I hope Jenna does well.

ACT TWO

As the announcement for showtime start begins, I try to focus on the show itself. And wow, what a show! When Jenna appears on stage, the audience seems to hold a collective breath.

She's in clear costume makeup and her outfit matches the high school setting, but she still looks amazing, even in the casual clothes.

And her voice...what a voice. At her solo moment, I have goosebumps. If I was allowed to record, I'd grab my phone and take a video. Not for me, but for her. So she could see how phenomenal she is.

As she walks off stage for intermission, she glances my way and my heart clenches. I'm sure it's only a coincidence but the rational part of my brain checked out the moment I saw her.

The show ends with a roaring standing ovation and, when she comes on to do her bow, I join in the various whoops and hollers.

A person seated behind me calls out, "So proud of you!" and I don't stop myself from turning around curiously. I immediately recognize Jenna's sister and mom from my Instagram stalking.

Our...situation...never got so far as to meeting them, but I've heard a lot about them and I smile politely as her sister glances at me.

When the actors all walk offstage and the show lights come on, I kneel down to grab my jacket, which is hanging off the plush velvet chair. A tap on my shoulder interrupts my reach for my purse.

"Gabriella, right?"

It's Jenna's sister, of course. I don't know her exact age but it seems she can't be more than a few years older than me. She has the same blonde hair, but where Jenna's face is all smiles and softness, her features are more stern and serious.

"Yes..." I'm unsure exactly what to say or ask.

"Jenna told us you'd be here. I'm Maddy, her sister." She reaches her hand out to shake and suddenly I feel as if I'm at a job interview.

13

What did she tell her sister about me? I don't want to think about it.

"Donna," the woman next to Maddy says. An older, more elegant version of Maddy. Clearly, Jenna's mother.

"Nice to meet you."

"Are you waiting to congratulate Jenna? You're welcome to join us."

Jenna and I didn't discuss the logistics of the happy hour drink, so perhaps it would be better to find her here first.

"That would be nice, thank you so much. I have to admit I've never met anyone who's worked in the theatre other than Jenna, so I have no idea where to find her."

"Us either, but I'm sure the staff could help."

Maddy ends up being correct and a helpful usher leads us to a lounge that acts as a waiting area. I recognize the other actors, even bundled up in their jackets and scarves, as they enter the room to greet their loved ones. The actor playing Regina is especially memorable and I resist the urge to go over and compliment her high note.

"What did you think of the show?" Donna asks me.

"It was really good. The stage design and direction were especially memorable. I haven't seen it before and it was interesting to see the adaptation from the movie to the stage. And of course, everyone's singing was fantastic."

Donna and Maddy nod appreciatively.

"Was this your first time seeing her perform?" Maddy asks.

I hesitate for a moment before responding. It's been a while since I've met any...person's parents and I don't want to say something uneasy.

"Yes. I like live entertainment but my work keeps me too busy most of the time, and I'm more of a homebody."

Maddy is about to respond when someone tackles her from behind.

"You're here!" Jenna exclaims and detaches herself to go hug her mom next.

It's extremely adorable and I push away the hint of disappointment that I'm not included in the hugging festivities.

"You were wonderful, darling." Donna tells her.

"Your Mirvish debut was a success, congratulations," Maddy chimes in.

"Just phenomenal," I add.

Jenna finally turns her attention to me and, God, I always forget how beautiful she is. Not in her physical features or stature but in her eyes. The warmth in them always makes me weak at the knees.

"Thank you for coming," she tells me earnestly.

"Of course, you know I've always supported you."

I hope I sound kind, and not pained, but my tone of voice could use some work (as Tyler notes helpfully anytime I unintentionally offend him with my curt manner).

"I'd love to stay, sweetie, but we have a long drive out of the city ahead of us," Maddy says after clearing her throat.

Great, that definitely didn't land how I meant it.

"Of course, I appreciate you being here." Jenna gives them both one last hug and, after a few more minutes of compliments and some inside jokes I don't quite understand, her family leaves.

Her attention turns back to me and I'm reminded of why it was so painful to let her go. It's like standing in the warm glow of the sun and I know I'll find it hard to resist. I try to stop these thoughts.

"So, where's this taco place?"

Jenna hooks her hand through my arm and I'm grateful for the barriers our jackets provide.

"Just a short walk, let's go."

I let her lead me out of the building (where several more folks stop us along the way, showering her with compliments and well-wishes) and we begin our walk along King Street.

"I love how, no matter what time it is, this street is always packed," Jenna says. "Makes me feel like I'm not delusional for being out past eleven."

"Oh my god, it's so late, will the happy hour even still be running?"

Jenna laughs. "I always forget how much of a planner you are. Yes, don't worry, they're open until three and the happy hour ends at midnight. Xavier, Artie's partner, is a bartender there, so they saved us a table."

"Artie?"

"He's one of the other understudies. He wasn't on tonight, but we rehearse together a lot. He's wonderful."

"That's awesome. Seriously, I'm so happy for you. You must be having a great time, meeting all these talented folks and growing your network, so to speak."

Jenna hums thoughtfully and snuggles closer as we wait at a light to cross the street.

"What about you? How's everything been?"

"The same. Work is still hectic but when will it ever not be? I did get that promotion, though. I'm not sure if being a manager is for me, but I'm liking the pay."

"Corporate is so interesting. Isn't this the time when you would normally job hop to another company?"

The light changes and we continue our walk over to the restaurant, talking about the different fields. Even though the topic itself isn't exactly riveting, I love how natural it is to talk to Jenna. I can't remember the last time it was this easy to just talk to someone.

By the time we make it past the thick crowd waiting to enter the restaurant and be seated, we have moved on to the topic of her work. I didn't intend to ask this outright but I decide that, if we're going to have a chance of being friends, I at least have to know.

"So, how long are you back for this time?"

"I'm not quite sure." She fiddles with a napkin. "I've missed having a place to call home, and my family. I think it'd be nice to be somewhere more permanently."

I'm about to reply when the server comes over.

"Hey, hey! Artie told me y'all would be coming by. First drink's on me," they say.

I'm thankful for the interruption. I'm not sure I can quite process what I've heard. I've been guarding my heart for an inevitable departure again, so to find out it may not come to pass is interesting.

After placing our order, I turn back to Jenna. One of my favourite things about her is her expressive features and the look in her eyes tells me she's nervous. It's not a look I see often.

"I get what you mean about having a permanent place. It's nice to have a 'home base' of sorts, and you seem really close with your family."

The mention of her family cheers her up.

"I really am. I can't believe they came all the way from Aurora to see me."

"You were amazing, I'm sure they'd come even from Barrie, if needed."

Jenna bats an eyelash. "Oh, really? How amazing was I? Tell me more." She leans forwards and cups her face in her hands, exaggerating her gestures.

"Oh, stop. You know how good you were."

"Just in the show?" She winks.

I almost choke on air. I clear my throat instead, hoping the dim lighting and makeup will hide the blush I can feel appearing.

Before I can think of a witty response, the server returns with our drinks.

Thankfully, the conversation pivots back to more harmless territory (Jenna's Toronto bucket list) and I'm in good spirits by the time the meal ends. Thank goodness for cheap drinks and delicious $3 tacos.

I pay for the meal as part of my congratulations for her big debut and we head out into the cold night.

Despite it being this late, the street is still busy with people going from place to place. I watch as people leaving the club across the street stumble out.

"Which way are you heading?" I ask. "I don't think you told me where your new place is."

"I'm about a fifteen-minute walk away. I got lucky, being this close to the theatre."

"You did." I put my hands in my pockets to warm them up.

Jenna smiles and hooks her arm through mine again. "C'mon, I'll walk you to the streetcar."

"Sure," I smile.

"I'd invite you over but my place is currently a mess. I'm still trying to sort out all the stuff I brought out from my storage unit. I forgot how much stuff I own. Living on a cruise ship for a year will do that."

My heart stumbles over the almost invitation and I force myself to adjust to the topic at hand.

"Moving is actually the worst. It's probably for the best, since I'm out way past my bedtime anyway—I have an early meeting tomorrow."

"Thanks for joining me to celebrate anyway."

"Any time." I really mean it, and that's the scary part.

We continue our walk in comfortable silence and I'm grateful for the one drink I had that's keeping me warm. As we get to the streetcar stop, I realize I don't want this to be the last time I see Jenna.

"What are you doing on the weekend? Maybe I can help you with some of that unpacking," I offer.

"Really? I'd love that." She smiles wide. She starts to say something else but the chime of an incoming streetcar distracts her.

"Get home safe, text me when you arrive."

The streetcar doors open next to us and, before I can react, she kisses me on the cheek.

"Thank you for tonight, it was special. Now go!"

She says the last part more forcefully as she playfully pushes me in the direction of the door. I manage to make it onto the streetcar (stopping at the doors to tap to pay) and I watch as she waves from the street as it pulls away.

Deep breaths, Gabriella.

All my attempts to stop myself from being pulled into her orbit are wiped away with that moment. The logical part of me wants to run away, shield myself from any hurt, but a bigger part of me—the part of me that fell for her the first time—wants it to happen again. Wants more.

On Saturday morning, I find myself waiting to be buzzed up to Jenna's apartment. I spent all of yesterday oscillating between panic, regret, optimism, and daydreaming. The usual songs about love made me think of her but so did the ones about cruel breakups. Oh God, this is why I usually stick to my code and my books. Real-life romance is not for the faint of heart, and I don't know if mine is strong enough to withstand another break.

Before I can talk myself out of it, I press the buzzer. One eerily silent elevator ride later, I'm in front of her door.

I knock.

Jenna's wearing sweatpants and an athletic top that clearly looks like it was meant for the gym. Her hair is tied up in a precise bun that would make Ariana Grande seethe with envy and, of course, there's her smile.

"Oh my gosh, thank you so much for coming over to help."

She continues to ramble as I enter the place. Cardboard boxes are stacked in the corner of the open-concept apartment, next to the couch. There are other large pieces of furniture around the place but the usual furnishings like books on the shelves or papers on the small office desk in the corner are missing.

"Please excuse the mess. I've unpacked a few boxes, but I haven't had time to go through everything. Thank goodness I can get by with the clothes from my suitcase and whatever Maddy was kind enough to lend me."

"No problem." I hang my jacket up on the hooks placed above the full-length mirror at the entrance.

I take a moment to examine myself in the process; the wind clearly did a number on my hair. *Oof.* I try to smooth it down as I follow Jenna further in but the apartment itself is a bit small compared to the place I rent and there's not much to see beyond the first glance.

"This is it." She does a theatrical ta-da flourish. "The bedroom is behind this door to the left and the washroom is to the right of the entrance. It's a bit small but it was the best I could do right now."

"I've seen worse," I honestly admit. "This place is a good size. Is this your previous couch or a new one?"

"Good eye. It's new but in that same grey colour."

"No wonder it looked a bit familiar." I nod thoughtfully as I try to avoid thinking about the things that happened on her last couch.

She seems to be thinking the same because she replies, "That couch saw some things...probably best to get a new one."

I nod thoughtfully.

"So, let's get started?"

Hours later, we plop onto the couch. I'm sweatier than I expected to be but we've made great progress, having unpacked and sorted most of Jenna's clothes, books, vinyls, and many knick-knacks. She's also started making a pile of things to either sell, donate, or give away, which includes a few old costumes and some books she no longer has interest in.

In our unpacking, I managed to find an old hoodie of mine that I mysteriously lost about a month before she left. I hold it up now and examine it.

"I still can't believe you had this."

"Of course! The best part of hooking up with someone is stealing their clothes."

I turn to face her, but she's looking towards her bedroom door, avoiding my gaze.

"That's all it was to you?" The hurt in my voice must creep through because Jenna turns to me, alarmed.

"Of course not."

I take a deep breath and put down the sweater. I hate confrontation and I hate talking about my feelings but not being fully open in the past is what has hurt the most and, if I'm going to get my heart broken again, at least I may as well rip the Band-Aid off.

"Then why didn't you say anything?"

Jenna moves closer and I sit up slightly to face her properly.

"Oh, Gabs...why didn't you?"

"I wanted to. I did. But how could I have, when you had these amazing opportunities waiting for you?"

"Still, it would've been nice to know." Jenna grabs my hand. "For what it's worth, I was really into you too."

"I would've done anything for you." It's nice talking to her like this, being open.

I squeeze her hand and she lightly strokes her thumb across my palm.

"And what about now?" she whispers, coming closer.

I search her eyes and I see the same person I fell for. I wonder if she still kisses the same way, fully open and needy. I decide to find out. I avoid her question for now with one of my own.

"Can I kiss you?"

Instead of replying, she moves in and kisses me first. It's almost better than I remember and she seems to agree as she moans a little when I tug on her lower lip.

She breaks away.

"You were always so good at that." She clutches my shoulders and searches my eyes.

I've missed seeing her this way and my throat almost closes with emotion at being in this situation again. I clear my throat and focus on another one of my goals.

"I was good at a lot of things." I move closer to her, pressing against her chest so I can lean into her ear.

"I wonder if you still taste just as delicious," I whisper and kiss the side of her neck.

She curls her arms behind my neck and raises her chin so I have better access.

"Please feel free to find out."

I laugh and continue my exploration, moving from her neck back to her chin and up to her mouth again. By the time we're kissing again, she's found her way into my lap, where she bounces against me every so often. As I move to lift her shirt, she stops me.

"You're killing me. This is so unfair," she pouts. I kiss it off her lips.

"In what way?"

"I was going to kiss you first, beg to see you like this and on my bed."

"You can still do that," I smile.

She takes a deep breath and kisses me, and I let her take control. She was always good at this too.

"Sweet, beautiful, analytical Gabs... Come to the bedroom with me."

"That isn't begging," I tease.

She huffs and kisses my neck, reaching for the bottom of my T-shirt to lift it up. I let her.

"Of course, you're wearing your beautiful lace. Please let me see if you have matching underwear on."

"Getting closer." I smile again at her obvious frustration.

"Pretty please." She raises her voice an octave and, normally, I would find near-whining annoying, but it's strangely endearing coming from her.

I stay silent but kiss her gently. She accepts the kiss before moving away so she can kiss my neck again. She makes her way down to my clavicle and lower down my chest. I lift off the couch slightly to give her better access, but she surprises me by moving back to my mouth. After a few more minutes that end with a tortured moan from me, she moves to whisper in my ear.

"Will you please let me make you come?"

"Absolutely," I reply instantly, forgetting the game we were playing.

She laughs and gently eases herself off my lap and stands. She holds out a hand and I grab it, letting her lift me off the couch.

She leads me to the bedroom where she quickly lays me down before crawling on top of me.

So sexy.

"Thank you, but I think I should be saying that to you."

"I didn't realize I said that out loud." I giggle.

She removes her own shirt and the playfulness dies down again.

"I can say it again... I could look at you forever," I admit.

She kisses me frantically in response and I let her take over. When she asks permission to use her fingers, I give it willingly and it doesn't take long for her to fulfill her promise. In return, I offer to investigate my own question. Afterwards, we lie naked together under her sheets, where I attempt to get more warmth now that the rush of the sex has faded slightly. She has always kept her apartment cold, and it doesn't take long to get goosebumps from the chill.

Despite being the larger of the pair, I tuck myself into her side. I always enjoyed being the little spoon.

"I can confirm that you indeed taste just as great as you did before," I tell her dreamily, once semi-rational thought returns.

She laughs and pulls me in closer. She pecks the top of my head.

"I love how cute you get when you're vulnerable. Your closed-off self is so different."

I try not to bristle under the scrutiny. "It's a defence mechanism. Push people away and they can't hurt me."

Jenna hums thoughtfully.

"I can see that. Well...thank you for being open with me today. I really did mean what I said; leaving you wasn't easy for me."

"It wasn't easy for me either. I know I told you to go. I could never be the one to ask you to choose me over a career, but it hurt."

"I know, my darling, I know."

I sit up and turn to face her. I forgot how beautiful she looks in these moments and I lean down to kiss her gently.

"I can't make you any promises," I say, "but at least I'll make sure to communicate more clearly. I know I get closed off when I sense incoming hurt, but I'll try to be better."

Jenna reaches up for a kiss and I bend down to meet her.

"I'll do the same. Anything for you, Gabs."

We take a break to order food but most of the rest of the day is spent in bed, reminiscing over old memories and trying to make new ones. I spent most of last year trying to forget Jenna, not because she was awful but because she was too great and I could see how she'd fit too perfectly in my life.

I spent so much of last year in regret for how things ended, for not being honest about what she meant to me. Even if I get hurt again, at least I'll be able to say that I won't regret what I did. My therapist would be so proud.

By the time I make it home on Sunday evening, I'm practically floating as I walk into my place. I didn't intend on staying over but it's hard to say no to Jenna and I couldn't find a logical reason as to why I should've refused.

I text Jenna to let her know that I've made it home safely (the sun setting at 5pm makes everyone in the city instantly more safety-prone) and, as I start preparing to make dinner and meal prep for the week, Leslie calls me.

"Hey, haven't heard from you in a while, everything okay?" I ask.

Leslie and I have one of those friendships where we may not text for a while but, as soon as we catch up, it's as if we haven't spent any time apart. The last I heard from her was before March break, which is usually when she gets too overwhelmed with childcare to talk regularly.

"Yes, I'm fine. I actually wanted to check in with you because I saw that Jenna was back in town and I missed that group call with you and Tyler. Before you get mad about me stalking your ex, I started following her from a Finsta account when you broke up so

I could keep tabs on her. Oh, and obviously I missed you, of course."

"I'm not upset, thanks for looking out for me." I put the phone on speaker as I continue moving around the kitchen. "I missed you too. How's John and Cass?"

"Cass is a sweet little angel. She and John are watching Coco for the fiftieth time so I thought I'd use the moment to escape so we can talk, as I know you're usually meal prepping now. Ah, there's the sound of the sink running."

"Yep, boiling some pasta for the next few lunches."

"You're hardcore. The thought of eating the same thing five meals in a row fills me with existential dread."

"You have fancy chef John to help you and I only have me, so..." I chuckle good-naturedly.

"Speaking of only you, how are you doing with everything?"

"Fine... I just got home from Jenna's." I'm thankful for the regular call so Leslie can't see the wide grin on my face.

She lets out a blood-curdling scream on the other end.

"Gabriella Marie Adams, when were you going to tell me? What does this mean? Are y'all back together?"

I laugh.

"I just got home so I'm telling you now. It's hard to provide updates when you spend all day making out...amongst other things."

Leslie lets out a gasp before continuing dramatically. "I cannot believe you right now. I mean, I love this for you but I'm a little shocked. I know how much you were hurt by her leaving. I don't want to see that again."

I can't fault her for thinking that way. She and Tyler were there for me last year when I was in the thick of heartbreak, only getting up to work to distract myself from the memories. I weirdly have to thank that time for the impressive promotion I got at work—at least it allowed me to afford all the chocolate and ice cream I could ever want.

"I know, I always appreciate everything you do for me and

how you took care of me when I couldn't take care of myself. I miss little C around here. Can you bring her over for a sleepover with her favourite auntie sometime soon?"

"That sounds like a great idea. I'll coordinate something with John soon. I'm sure he'd like to have a boy's weekend so they can do something boring like a *Lord of the Rings* marathon."

"Don't knock Legolas like that so innocently. It's not John's fault you just have no taste."

I can practically hear Leslie roll her eyes. "Fine, fine. I forgot who I'm talking to. But seriously... You're okay, right?"

"Yes, I'm doing okay. Great, even. I know it's a little messed up but I'm feeling okay with this. We had a good conversation and I don't think everything is magically fixed, but I'm feeling optimistic about it; and you know that's a rare feeling for me."

Leslie hums thoughtfully. "Well, I'm happy for you but a little worried. Promise you'll keep me updated if you even think about renting a U-Haul together?"

I laugh so hard, I startle myself.

"Absolutely, you'll be the first to know."

"Good... Now, how was the weekend, hmm?"

Before I can respond, I hear a little commotion in the background and then C's adorable three-year-old voice breaks through.

"Auntie Gabriella, hiiiiii," she sing-songs. "When will you come visit?"

"Very soon, I promise."

We chat for a few minutes (mainly me listening while she tells me about the movie she's watching and the picture she's drawing) and then Leslie interrupts her.

"Thanks, sweetie, but it's late and Auntie Gabriella needs her beauty sleep, say bye," she says in the adorable voice she reserves for her precious baby.

C signs off and I say my goodbyes to Leslie, promising to arrange something soon for all of us (including Tyler) to meet.

I spend the rest of the evening in a great mood and, when I send a picture over of my meal to Jenna, she responds with her usual loving disdain for my "freakish habits"—her words, not mine.

CHAPTER FOUR

In the few weeks that Jenna has been back in town, we've accomplished many of the typical date-things to do in the city. On a weekend where she has to perform twice, I keep her company while she does warm-up and uses a fancy machine to steam her vocal chords. Mainly, I just watch in awe as she does her thing and I sing her praises. Later, when she performs her solo and looks towards me in the audience, I feel more and more of my armour chip away for her.

We also visit the Distillery District and take a cheesy photo in front of the large heart sign. She posts it to her Instagram and I spend at least 24 hours panicking about what it means for our relationship (assuming it is one). The caption is full of random red emojis, revealing nothing, and while my friends and I do our best to try and identify what it may mean, we decide to let it be. The comments are thankfully all supportive and I also do my best not to cyberstalk all the comments from people who seem to be her castmates.

On a Friday night, a few days after my internal Instagram debacle, we are snuggled together on my couch. It has a pull-out function that I tend to keep permanently in place as there's nothing quite like always being able to lie down on the couch.

Jenna loves this logic and we may have spent some time doing something more than just lying down.

She's tucked into my side while Netflix automatically queues up the second episode of a particularly bland show we were watching, just for the sake of watching something. I don't really care what it is specifically; I just enjoy her company.

She turns to me, interrupting the way I was playing with her hair.

"What are you doing this weekend?"

"Oh, Leslie and her daughter are coming over for a sleepover, and Tyler too."

"That sounds like fun! I know how much you love them all. You'll have a great weekend." She seems satisfied by my answer because she turns back to the TV.

"What about you?"

She snuggles closer into me, resting her head on my shoulder.

"I have a matinee show tomorrow and another one on Sunday. I don't think I'm playing the lead again, likely just one song, but I really should be at home resting my voice."

"That's fair... I really want to make an innuendo about how we can do something that doesn't require your voice but first, I think I'd love for you to join us for dinner tomorrow. If you can, of course."

Jenna detaches herself again to sit up.

"Really? Are you sure?"

I nod and give her a small peck on the mouth.

"Yes, I want them to get to know you. It won't be easy but they're an important part of my life and so are you."

Jenna smiles.

"You're important in my life too." She bends down to kiss me and I willingly oblige.

Just as I start to deepen the kiss, she sits up with a mischievous look in her eye.

"Absolutely, I will be here tomorrow after my show if I can.

But, can we get back to the part where we were going to do something that doesn't require speaking?"

I laugh and tug her back to me. "Definitely... Thank you for wanting to be here and for wanting to meet them." I reward her with a kiss.

"Wouldn't want to be anywhere else," she responds between kisses. I silently agree.

∼

Tyler arrives first the next day, 2L Sprite bottle in hand and a pack of pencil crayons in the other.

"Wow, Uncle Tyler really came to slay today," I say as I open the door for him.

He rolls his eyes and walks past me into the house.

"Nate also said that to me on my way out. I forget when we started to say 'slay' non-ironically."

"Nate?" I do my best to waggle an eyebrow at him but I'm sure it just turns out strange as he bursts into laughter instead.

"Never do that again, please."

"Crappy facial expression aside, answer the question." I lower my voice in a mock threat.

"You know... Nate... The guy I've been seeing."

I scream. "No, I did not know! Leslie is going to be so pissed when she finds out."

"There's nothing to find out or uncover. He's just a nice guy. A librarian."

"A librarian? How sexy," I joke.

"Actually, yes." Tyler winks.

I raise my eyebrow curiously. Just as I contemplate asking for details, the doorbell rings.

I let Leslie and the adorable Cass in, and C promptly starts telling me about her adventures on the subway.

"Wow, the subway! Doesn't it go so fast?" I say to her in a voice I reserve exclusively for my friends' children.

Cass and I make idle chitchat like this for a few minutes while Tyler and Leslie have a moment to catch up.

Thirty minutes later, the adults are spread out on the couch while Cass braids my hair as we sit on the floor. Her version of braiding is more like grabbing fistfuls of hair and moving them side to side behind my back but I don't mind. I glance at the clock on the oven and silently curse.

"Cass, let's take a break. I need to share something important with your mom."

"A secret?"

"No, not a secret. You can listen." I ruffle her hair as she stares at me in confusion.

"Do you want to watch a movie?" I offer to the group, but with Cass present, it ends up being an animated one.

As the movie starts and Cass jumps up onto the couch to watch it, I beckon Tyler and Leslie over to the kitchen.

"Glass of wine?" I offer, hoping to butter them up a bit.

"You know I won't refuse," Leslie says, standing at the kitchen island.

I pour three glasses but remove a fourth glass from the cupboard and leave it out. I see Leslie eyeing it suspiciously, but she says nothing as we do a first cheers to good friendships.

"So... First, no one get mad."

Tyler rolls his eyes. "Just spit it out, this secrecy shit isn't you."

"Fine, fine... I invited Jenna to come by tonight for dinner."

Leslie puts down her glass and I turn to her in panic.

"I know, I know. But Leslie, I'm so happy right now. I want her to meet you both, properly."

"That's fair, but I would've appreciated a head's up so I could warn Cass."

I feel like an idiot. Leslie must read the look on my face because she comes over to me.

"It's okay, I trust you. Just don't let her, or you, get too attached. I want to support you, I really do, but I saw what happened when it didn't work out."

"Thanks." I take a sip of wine and try to calm down from the new impending anxiety that has taken over at the thought of something going wrong.

"No need for all that, Gabriella." Tyler has always been a pro at reading my facial expressions.

He walks over to give me a hug.

"I'm obviously worried about it not working out, too," I say, "but for now... It's been so fun and nice and I'm happy. Really."

Leslie gives me a hug too.

"As long as you're happy, we're happy."

A small body tumbles into my legs, and Cass calls out, "Auntie Gabriella, don't be sad. We love you!"

I detach myself from Leslie and Tyler to pick her up.

"I'm not sad, I'm so happy I have the best little nibling in the world." I tickle her for emphasis.

Just then, the doorbell rings.

"Who is it?" Cass asks, her large eyes open and curious.

"My friend, want to go meet her?"

Cass nods enthusiastically and I carry her with me to get the door.

Jenna blinks in surprise at me holding a child but she greets Cass with a wide smile.

"Hey! And this must be the fabulous C I've heard so much about?"

"You know me?" Cass asks, wondrous.

Jenna and I chuckle as I move back to let her in. She walks in and closes the door behind her.

"No, no, I've just heard good things," she clarifies.

"Auntie, put me down. I want to show... Wait, what's your name?"

"I'm Jenna, it's nice to meet you."

"I want to show Auntie Jenna my toys," Cass tells me.

I comply with her request and Cass promptly grabs Jenna's hand to drag her to my living room, where she set up her stuffed plushies earlier.

I put away Jenna's jacket and head back to the kitchen to join Tyler and Leslie, who are watching this new development curiously.

"At least she's good with kids," Leslie says, finishing up her wine glass.

"Cass really wasted no time. I think she's describing what she wants for her birthday," Tyler chimes in.

I take a sip of my wine. Seeing Cass and Jenna interacting fills my heart with a warmth I hadn't anticipated. For a brief moment, I let my mind wander to the future and what a similar moment would look like with someone else's children... Perhaps ours...

I force myself to stop the thought. There's no point daydreaming just yet, but damn, Jenna would make a great parent.

Tyler turns to me with his uncanny way of reading my face.

"Guard your ovaries, woman."

"Oh my god, you're so dramatic."

"Speaking of drama, Cass looks about ready to put on a play for us with all those stuffies." Leslie wanders back over to the area where Jenna and Cass are playing. She pauses the now-forgotten movie playing in the background.

"C, how about we help Auntie Gabriella place a pizza order?"

"Pizza!!" Cass yells, forgetting entirely about her new friend.

While Leslie and I set about ordering food, I can see Tyler chatting with Jenna out of the corner of my eye. They're both giggling and I'm relieved to see it. It's not that I thought they wouldn't get along but it's a relief to see that things are not as disastrous as my mind thought they might be.

When we rejoin them, Jenna looks my way for the first time this evening and I can't help but smile at her. Ugh. I'm a smitten kitten. And I know it.

We agree on a different movie to watch and I end up on the corner of the couch closest to the door (so I can run over to grab the pizza when it arrives) and Jenna sits next to me, Cass on her other side.

As the movie starts, Jenna grabs my hand and snuggles into my side. I shift a little so she's more comfortable against my shoulder, and if my friends weren't all here (as much as I love them), this would be the perfect date night. When the doorbell rings, Jenna joins me to answer the door and she assists in grabbing the boxes from the delivery person's outstretched hands.

I pay and Jenna brings the boxes over to the kitchen.

"Pizza's here!" she announces as I grab plates from the cupboards.

Everyone runs over to grab their slices and Tyler, Leslie, and Cass all head back to the couch in no time. I'm about to join them when Jenna stops me. She grabs the plate out of my hand and places it back on the kitchen island.

"Let's go talk for a second." She leads me into the bathroom where she closes the door behind me.

Pushed against the door, I turn to her.

"We really should rejoin the group," I whisper, powerlessly. It's pointless to resist but I try to employ some logic.

The look in her eye tells me she definitely has more than just talking planned, and my suspicion is confirmed when she kisses me.

I let her control the kiss, loving how needy she seems. When she pushes her leg between mine, I force myself to pull away.

"Babe, we really shouldn't."

She gives me one more peck and reluctantly lays her forehead on my shoulder, breathing out.

"I know, I know. When I saw you holding Cass at the door, something overcame me. You just looked so sexy."

This time, it's her words that make my heart race in anticipation.

"How do you think I felt watching you playing with her?" I gently stroke her hair and exhale.

She raises her head again, searching my face.

"Really?"

The look in her eye is so hopeful, so vulnerable, that I have no choice but to kiss her again. Really, I have no choice.

Just as I start to mull reaching over to unbutton her pants, a small voice calls out.

"Auntie, your pizza is getting cold!"

Jenna pulls away and turns to look in the mirror.

"Coming!" she calls out in response.

I exhale again, trying to get my heartbeat back to an acceptable rate. I shake my head to try and clear the escalating thoughts.

Jenna turns to me and begins straightening my T-shirt.

"God, I wish we could be doing the other kind of coming."

I snort a laugh. "You're ridiculous." I give her another peck and whisper, "Later."

Before she has time to react, I exit the bathroom and head back to the kitchen. I grab our plates and move to the couch. Jenna joins me there.

The rest of the evening passes calmly, and my heart warms every time I see Jenna interacting with my closest friends. Seeing the person I *like* getting along with my chosen family affects me in a way I hadn't anticipated, and though my heart is warm with joy, a small part of my mind can't help but worry that this bliss won't last. After our third movie and an endless pile of snacks, I check my phone (which has been sitting neglected as all the people I'd probably text are here) and startle at the time.

"Okay, friends, it's past midnight. I think we need to get ready for bed," I announce, much to Cass's obvious chagrin.

"Auntie Gabriella is right, my love." Leslie picks up Cass and snuggles her close to her chest. "Let's go brush our teeth and get comfy in the large bed Auntie G set up for us."

Cass sighs, but before she can fight, a yawn slips out. Tyler yawns too.

"Oh yeah, I'm feeling it." He stands and stretches. "I'll set up the pull-out couch, so you can walk Jenna out."

While the rest of the guests begin their nighttime routine, I wait with Jenna outside on the porch for her ride home.

"I wish you could stay too, but there's not enough room."

"I understand." She seems sincere and I try to let my guilt about it dissipate.

"Come here." She holds out her arms and I don't hesitate to wrap myself up in them.

While there's only a slight chill in the air, I find it more comforting than warming. A gust of wind nearly blows her over and I change my mind about it being only slightly chilly.

After a comfortable few seconds of silence, I pull away slightly so I can look her in the eyes. I could lose myself in them.

"What time is your Uber expected to arrive?" I ask. "Perhaps we should've waited inside. I don't want you to freeze."

"It's okay, I don't mind waiting out here. Now I can continue what we started in the bathroom."

I welcome her kiss, and though it's sweet, I try to pour in everything I'm feeling at the moment. The admiration I have for her, the joy I have at seeing her interacting with the people closest to me, how I wish she could stay.

She pulls away, her cheeks red in a way that I can't tell whether it's from the cold or from our kiss.

"Babe, you're killing me." She rests her head on my shoulder. "I wish I could take you home with me."

I laugh.

"And just leave my houseguests behind to fend for themselves?"

"Tyler seems perfectly capable of taking care of your place in your absence."

"I'm sure he is," I chuckle. "We'll find another time, promise."

Jenna smiles at that and snuggles closer to me. She detaches one arm to check her phone.

"Three minutes," she announces.

I hum in acknowledgement.

"Well, thank you for being here tonight. I know your schedule is packed right now but it was nice seeing you with everyone. What did you think?"

"Thanks for having me, silly. I had fun. Leslie doesn't warm up easy but I think I won her over in the end. Tyler is a sweetheart, as I knew he would be."

Before I can overthink too much about this or ask more questions, a silver car pulls up. On a quiet residential street like this, it's pretty easy to spot.

"I think that's my Uber." Jenna pecks me on the cheek and runs off.

"Good night, I'll text you when I get home!" she calls out as she runs towards the back of the car, checking its license plate. One confirmed, she hops into the backseat. With a final wave, she's gone.

When I go back inside, the lights are all off, except one lamp in the living room. I remove my jacket quietly in an attempt not to disturb Tyler, who's lying on one half of the fold-out couch under the large duvet I made sure to wash in advance.

As I get closer and get under the covers, I realize he's scrolling on his phone. The light from the tiny screen lights up his face and I smile as he turns to me.

"So, successful day?"

"Yes... What did you think?"

"She seems nice. Both of you seem wild about each other."

I smile at that.

"Both of us?"

Tyler playfully pushes me. "Yes, you ingrate. Your situationship seems to be much more than that."

The thought warms me and I lay a hand under my head so I can see him better.

"What about you and your situation? Do you think you're moving in that direction?"

Tyler smiles. "Maybe. It's hard to say. We're not like you lesbians, we don't have the movers on standby or anything."

"Oh, shut up." I roll my eyes.

"Seriously, I'm happy for you. I was a little nervous and I'm still a bit worried that you'll get your heart broken, but it's also nice seeing you so happy. And having something to do other than work all the time," he says.

"I don't work all the time," I retort.

"I don't know about that... We were worried about you for a while."

I exhale and turn to stare at the ceiling. I understand what he's saying, and looking back, I probably didn't handle my emotions as well as I could have.

"It was a hard time," I finally admit. "But I don't regret it. Not because we have something now but because I was happy while it lasted and I learned a lot about myself. What's the saying? Better to have loved and lost..."

Tyler shoves me playfully. "Okay, miss philosopher, go off, I guess."

We chitchat for a few more minutes before I get too sleepy. As we drift off to sleep, I try to avoid thinking about the future and what it could mean.

CHAPTER FIVE

While the sleepover was a resounding success, it's a while before Jenna and I see each other in person again. With March break affecting actors' schedules, Jenna is called to perform almost every night. She doesn't mind the money (she earns extra when she actually performs) but I can tell the extra practices, vocal lessons, and sheer effort of giving it 120% on the stage are exhausting her. Her texts become curt, and while she posts cute 'behind-the-scenes' Instagram videos and TikToks, I can tell she's acting in them too. Her usual smile and bright eyes seem dull, worn out.

On Friday night, I wait outside the stage door with a bouquet of flowers. The timing has worked out in my favour as she ended up understudying for one of the other leads today—her first time playing this particular character. I could feel her nervous energy through the brief text she sent this morning to let me know.

I knock at the stage door and a gruff man opens it reluctantly.

"Can I help you?"

"I'm here for Jenna Daniels. A friend." I try to give my nicest 'I'm-not-a-stalker' smile.

"Name?"

"Gabriella."

"Okay, wait here." The door closes unceremoniously and I try not to let the cold affect me.

After a few minutes (in which I engage in an internal argument with myself about whether I'm being cute or creepy), the door opens and Jenna comes out. She's still in her stage makeup (thick foundation and interesting eyebrows) but she's bundled up in an oversized hoodie.

Just as she starts to greet me, the door opens further and a skinny man pokes his head out. His hair is slicked back and coiffed in the perfect f-boy look, and I quickly realize he must've been playing a member of the football team in the show.

"Oh, this is the girlfriend! So cute," he says.

Jenna rolls her eyes at him as she reaches for the flowers I'm holding. Right, flowers.

"Thank you, darling," Jenna says.

She tugs on my sleeve and I take her cue to step into the crowded basement-looking hallway. It's extremely narrow and I worry about bumping into something important, like those wires in the corner that I nearly trip over.

"This is Artie." Jenna gestures at the man, who gives an enthusiastic wave.

"Oh, yes, I remember. You helped us get the table at that restaurant."

Artie nods enthusiastically. The energy coming out of him is triple the amount I'd be able to muster this late at night but I chalk it up to some secret showbiz thing I'll never understand. That, and extroverts.

"Yes, I had to when I heard Jenna's story of her lost love, ugh, so romantic. You're even prettier than Jenna said."

"Thank you." I manage a light chuckle, despite the information overload.

Lost love? Jenna said I was pretty?

She must sense that the gears in my head are starting to turn curiously because she lets out an embarrassed giggle and begins to physically shove Artie back towards the dressing rooms.

"Haha, thank you, I'll see you at the next one," she says to him once they've moved far enough away for him to get the hint. With a sportsmanlike bow, Artie disappears into another room.

"Sorry about him, he can be a lot for 11pm on a Friday."

"It's okay, it's nice to meet your friends. And I'm happy to see you... Hi." I punctuate the greeting with a kiss to her cheek.

She smiles and turns to the bouquet she's holding, examining the flowers for a few moments.

"This is so sweet, thank you."

"You earned it with all these late nights and playing the lead... Wow. I'm in awe of you," I tell her honestly.

She turns to me with the sweetest expression. I want to frame it.

"Thank you. If I didn't have six layers of makeup on right now, I'd be all over you. Let me go wipe it off so you can come home with me to help me pick out a vase for the flowers."

"Just a vase for the flowers?" I tease.

"We can continue our conversation from your bathroom a few days ago." She winks and runs off before I can reply.

Well, at least I'm glad to know I'm not the only one who's been thinking about it.

I'm still smiling when she returns ten minutes later and she smiles back when she finally reaches me.

She kisses me tenderly, dropping her gym bag next to where I'm standing. Surprised, I return the kiss and reach for her waist, despite the jacket in my way. She grabs my lapels to pull me closer and I eagerly respond by tugging on her lower lip.

Several wolf whistles finally interrupt us and we break apart. I have to blink a few times to remember we're in her place of work.

Oops.

"I had to use almost an entire pack of makeup wipes but that was worth it," she giggles and gives me a short peck. She stands in front of me and I'm glad that she's blocking the passersby from my view.

She steps back and reaches for her duffel. She turns back to call out one last goodbye to her castmates and then leads me to the door.

The wind this evening is bitter, a remnant from an unusually long winter, and I shiver as the cold hits my face.

We agree on taking the streetcar to her place to avoid the worst of the cold and I grab her duffel for her, letting her get some rest after the long day she's had.

Like most Torontonians, we choose to ignore the nastiness of the TTC seats and sit down when we board the streetcar.

Jenna snuggles against me and I shift so she can rest on my shoulder more comfortably.

"Can you pick me up after every show? Flowers, holding my bag... A girl could get used to this," she sighs dreamily.

"Sure, whatever you want."

We sit in comfortable silence, and when the streetcar arrives at her stop, we both get off.

"Are you hungry?" she asks as we begin the short walk to her apartment building.

"No, it's so late already that I had dinner."

She hums in understanding and we continue our comfortable silence until we arrive at her building. She uses her fob to unlock the door and waves to the security guard as she passes.

"Have a good night," she calls to him cheerfully and he smiles, returning the greeting.

"Wow, I've never seen people in the city actually interact with security unless they have to."

"I try to be polite when I can," she says as we enter the elevator. "If something happens to me, I need there to be someone who notices."

"That's strangely cynical, but nice, I think." I'm not sure what to make of it.

"It comes in handy. They held my packages longer than the two-day maximum when I was at your place two weeks ago."

The elevator finally arrives on the 17th floor and we step out together. As she unlocks her door, a nervous energy fills me.

Though I know she's been busy lately, her place is surprisingly clean and I comment on it.

"Thank you. Cleaning relaxes me so I've been scrubbing in between lessons and trying not to strain my voice."

"Fair, fair." I make sure to leave my stuff carefully at the front entryway.

"Do you want some water?"

"Sure," I say. "My friends would say that's the sign of a great host, a beverage as soon as you walk through the door."

Jenna laughs as she opens the cupboard.

"Well, I'll be sure to thank them if they ever tell me that. Honestly, I'm trying very hard to seem normal right now."

"Are you tired after your show? We can just get comfy and you can get some rest. I'll have to borrow some pyjamas, though," I say as I take a seat at the bar stool at the island across from her small kitchen.

"No, no, I'm just thinking of the best way to rip your clothes off."

Thank God I didn't start drinking the water yet; otherwise I'd surely choke.

She places the glass in front of me and walks around the island to stand next to me. I turn to her.

"Wow, getting right into it?" I tease.

"What can I say? My girlfriend is extremely sexy and I've been thinking about it all day."

"Girlfriend?" I hope my voice doesn't sound as eager as it feels to me internally.

"Was that too cheesy a way to ask you?"

"Yes, but it's okay because I will absolutely be your girlfriend."

We smile at each other in ridiculous silence for a few moments before she tugs on my arm and pulls me towards the couch.

"Great, because I absolutely have some things planned for my new girlfriend."

"Lovely, because your new girlfriend is ready."

She gently pushes me down onto the couch where she climbs into my lap, straddling me.

"In a rush?" I giggle as I place a kiss on her neck.

"I've been thinking about it... First, the couch." She kisses me openly. "Then the bedroom." She interrupts herself to begin kissing my neck. "Maybe even the bathroom to shower, and then get right into it again. Repeat the cycle."

I try to respond but the idea, combined with her determined sucking on my neck, leaves me at a loss for words.

"Sounds like a plan," I finally manage to say when she pauses for a moment to look back into my eyes. I lean forwards and aim for her lips, hungrily tugging her closer towards me.

She deepens the kiss and it doesn't take long for clothes to go flying. She's in the middle of unhooking my bra when an intrusive thought appears.

"Do you have curtains? I suddenly feel like everyone outside can watch this happen."

"This high up, no one will be peeking. And if they are, then they're getting the best show in the city right now."

"No, I'm pretty sure the best show would be the one starring you earlier tonight."

Jenna leans back to stare at me for a moment.

"Too corny?" I ask.

"Definitely. But I'm trying to figure out why that made me even more horny."

I laugh before pulling her in for another kiss. She lets me take control and I soon find my hand caressing her soft silk underwear.

"Wait a moment." She stops my ravenous kissing of her neck with a light tug away.

"Let's continue this in the bedroom," she finally says.

"Are you sure? The audience out there may want to see this."

"I'm sure they would, but I want this to be only for us."

It's my turn to consider her statement carefully. I decide that I'm into it, though I decide to mentally file the audience observation idea for later.

Though my brain agrees, my hand continues its light caress and I'm rewarded with the feel of her wetness.

"Are you sure? I think you may want to continue things out here," I say, increasing the pace of my stroking.

It's almost as if I can see the inner battle playing out on her face—I can tell she wants to wrap it up, but instead of words, a moan escapes her mouth.

"C'mon, baby," I coax. "Come for me right here." I kiss her on the lips to deepen my point and she hungrily returns it. She breaks away after a moment.

"I'm close," she finally admits, whispering as her face reddens.

"Anything you need me to do?" I ask, adding my index finger into the mix. She moans in response and I feel her clench around me in response.

"That, more," she eventually adds. I smile and continue as instructed.

God, she looks so beautiful like this.

I tell her so and continue with the adorations until I am successful in my mission. I kiss her again as she comes down from her high and her breathing returns to normal.

"That is so unfair, I had the opposite planned." Jenna eventually says, her lighthearted tone not matching the intent behind the words.

"What a likely story."

"Well, there were all those other things on my list. What should we start with?"

"Bed, please," I request with a kiss. "Watching you has made me so close that you could probably just breath on me and I'd instantly come."

"Should we go test that out?" Jenna rises and holds out a hand for me to follow.

I follow her to the bedroom. She pauses to run into the bathroom to grab a hand towel, which I use to wipe my hand.

"My turn," she says as she snatches the towel out of my hands and places it on her nightstand. She gently pushes me onto the bed and begins the elegant work of removing my pants.

"Hands feel like too much work," she says matter-of-factly. "I'll just use my mouth."

"If you insist," I somehow manage to respond. The fact that I can even utter a sentence in this situation is impressive enough.

It doesn't take long for Jenna to turn me into a quivering mess, and when she's done with her ravaging, I don't hesitate to bring her in for a kiss. The taste of my own pleasure on her lips is new, but not unwelcome.

"Thank you," I sincerely say as we break apart.

She rests next to me and I brush the hair out of her eyes as she leans forwards to study my face.

"How did I live for so long without having these moments in my life? Without getting to see you like this?" she whispers.

The tenderness of the moment has me at a loss for words and I'm unsure how to reply; my usual banter fails to magically appear.

She must see something in my expression because her brows furrow.

"Sorry, was that too much?"

It's hard to capture this exact feeling I'm experiencing but I want to try.

"Yes, it's almost too much but also not enough. I don't know how exactly to say it but I'm in serious danger with you."

"Danger?" Jenna laughs, kissing my cheek. It's her turn to caress my hair as she waits on a response.

"Danger of falling in love," I settle on, hoping the tightness in my throat doesn't betray me.

I didn't have getting emotional on my to-do list for the evening—but her name was all over it so at least that's a plus in that column.

"You are so sweet, underneath all those walls you have up," Jenna responds and rewards me with eager kisses.

"I feel the same way," she eventually says as we finish out another round of activity that has both sweating.

CHAPTER SIX

It's hard to consider myself having a routine that doesn't revolve solely around work, but after the past few whirlwind weeks, I've gotten comfortable with having a more regular schedule that includes Jenna. Yes, there's the occasional changed dinner plan when Jenna is called in to work, but overall, I find those moments of flexibility interesting. Besides, Jenna's post-show high makes her adventurous, and I am not one to complain about that.

Today is really giving Monday energy, and it takes exactly three seconds from the end of a pointless meeting to pick up my phone and start scrolling. I'm aiming for a cute video as a distraction and am surprised by a text from Jenna.

> babe
>
> babe
>
> babe

>> yes?

> oh wow i thought you'd be working away at whatever it is you do... this derails my grand plan

ACT TWO

> sorry i needed the distraction from whatever it is that i do, i can disappear if that helps

wait no wait

let's go out for dinner today, my treat

> this feels like a set up for some reason, anything i need to prepare for?

just show up as your sexy normal self

okay i take that back - wear that matching bra underwear set i bought you

Jenna surprised me with it a week ago and it's remained hidden in my dresser ever since. For some reason, I've been wanting to save it for a special occasion, though I'm unsure of exactly what that special occasion would be. Anyone braver than me would've likely put it on to take a picture to send to her, just to clarify that it is indeed the set I'm picturing, of course. But I've never been one to send dirty pictures, and while the thought is tempting, I dismiss it.

> okay deal

Jenna and I chat for a bit longer as she finalizes some details about the exact nature of the dinner. The venue ends up being one I've always wanted to try, a vegan restaurant where the food doesn't taste like it's vegan, allegedly.

Heart pounding, I make it to the restaurant later that evening, wearing a comfortable pullover and jeans over Jenna's instructions. When I walk in, Jenna waves enthusiastically to me. She pulls me in for a quick peck and I can tell her level of excitement is high today, even for her.

"Wow, someone had a good day." I smile.

"It's about to be even better, I'm starving."

"Have you been here before? I've always wanted to try it."

"Yes, and their sushi specials are amazing. It tastes like actual sushi, surprisingly. Without the gross fish taste, of course."

I laugh at the weirdness of that sentence, trying to imagine exactly what she means. I'm about to respond when the server calls us over to show us to our table. When we sit down, the waitstaff arrives immediately to pour us a glass of water.

"Will you be participating in our Maki Monday special? Unlimited sushi for $27 each."

"This is why you offered to pay," I tease Jenna when we confirm that unlimited sushi does sound good, but we'll need to look at the selection before deciding.

"I had my reasons. That wasn't the only one, though." Jenna laughs good-naturedly.

I'm grateful that we've been seated at a booth and not the overcrowded main area of the restaurant because the comfortable moment gives me an excuse to reach across the table for her hand.

"So, what's the special occasion then, my dear?"

She squeezes my hand and uses her other hand to take a sip of water.

"Getting nervous over here," she says awkwardly. Her obvious anxiety starts to make me a little fidgety as well.

She takes a deep breath and opens her mouth to say something, when the waitstaff appears again.

"Know what you'd like to order?" they ask.

"Can you give us a few?" Jenna asks them.

The handholding across the table starts to feel awkward and I detach myself as the waitstaff walks away. I use my now-free hand to take a sip of water.

This is the most stiff we've been around each other lately and it unnerves me. I take a deep breath myself and look up to find Jenna's gaze fixed on me.

"So, what's this big news?" I ask, trying to sound cheerful.

"I'm going to Broadway, BROADWAY!" she exclaims.

It doesn't take faking cheerfulness for me to be excited for her.

"Oh my god. That is huge." I have a genuine smile on my face. "Do we need to order champagne for the table?"

Jenna reaches over for my hand again.

"No champagne necessary, I'm just happy you're happy for me."

"Of course, why wouldn't I be?"

I start laughing at the notion. *Of course, only good news for my girlf—*

"Because I have to move to New York," Jenna says, her description of reality interrupting my thoughts.

Ah, yes, reality. Another separation. No easy texting to see when the other is available. Thousands of kilometres separating us.

The conflict in my emotions must be written on my face because Jenna slides out of the booth to sit next to me on my side.

"It's okay, baby, we'll figure it out."

"I think I'm the one supposed to be saying that to you."

"I don't know all the Gabriella expressions yet but I'm pretty sure yours is code for 'help what do we do now'... probably because I'm thinking the same thing."

Before I can respond, the waitstaff appears again.

"Decided on which sushi you'd like?" they try more optimistically.

"Sure, can you give us four of your best rolls? Whatever you recommend." Jenna flashes them her usual customer service smile and they send the order via iPad before walking off.

The rest of the dinner passes by in awkward small talk, both of us attempting to ignore the looming overcast ahead. My thoughts oscillate between excitement and dread and I have to force myself to focus on the food in front of me. It helps that we're seated next to each other and I can only glance at her from the corner of my eye. After a silent minute as we wait for the waitstaff to bring over their payment machine, Jenna covers the bill and we head out of the restaurant, now making idle conversation about how unusually fast the rest of the service was.

Standing near the front entrance to the restaurant, we do that awkward milling around thing where you're both waiting for the other person to start talking or suggest a plan of action. In today's hustle and bustle, I forgot that I put on Jenna's present and the sensation of it starts to make me feel uneasy now that I don't know what the future holds.

"Do you want to come over, so we can talk? I don't want to end the night on this note," Jenna says in a rush before I have a moment to think.

I agree and we take the streetcar to her place, stopping for a bubble tea along the way. Though we're both actively ignoring the conversation ahead (or at least I am), I'm thankful for the light conversation about the different flavours. Even with this hanging over us, I find myself relaxing and telling her about my latest work worry and the meme that got me through my lunch hour. In return, she shares a hilarious rehearsal story and we take a selfie with our bubble teas. This is the benefit of being with someone who understands you; and it's with a bittersweet feeling that I realize this is exactly what I will miss.

By the time we make it back to her place, a range of thoughts have gone in and out of my brain with no real link to them.

Should we do long distance? But the distance is what caused us to stop seeing each other the first time... Yes, we're girlfriends now but we didn't really talk about what kind of commitment that actually means.

"Stop thinking so loud, I can feel it from here," Jenna calls over from the couch where she has already crossed her legs (her comfy position; my nightmare).

I smile and quickly hang up my jacket next to hers. I stop to grab my drink from where I left it on the counter upon entering.

"Was it really that loud?"

"Yes, it was. You don't do anything in half-measure, Gabs."

I'm about to reply, or at least attempt to, when she adds, "But it's okay, that's one of the many things I love about you."

"You love about me?" I manage to repeat back, parrot-like repetition being the only thing I can think of to say.

"You are as dense as you are beautiful." She kisses me on the cheek before taking another sip of her drink.

I watch her in awe for a few seconds before some thought actually kicks in.

Yes, beautiful.

I grab the drink from her hands and place it on the coffee table next to mine. I lean in for a kiss and it's sweet, thanks to the passionfruit flavour of her drink. I try to infuse the kiss with everything I'm feeling; the deep admiration I have for her and the fact that I'll miss her.

She pulls away after a few minutes.

"Wow, should we have bubble tea every day?"

I laugh initially but the feeling of elation from her words fades as my brain starts to remind me of the uncertainty up ahead. Jenna must read it on my face because she picks up her drink again and hands me mine. I take a sip of the milky tea before leaning back against the couch, turning to face the blank TV screen instead of her.

I hear Jenna shift and take a deep breath.

"Not having the hard conversations is what caused us to self-destruct last time. I don't want a repeat of that with you. I'll go first if it's easier."

As much as I would love for her to do that, I have to recognize that it would be taking the easy way out. One of the things my friends and I talked about last time is that I let things happen to me, instead of reaching out and taking action. If speaking about how I feel will help, maybe that's what I need to do.

"No, I'll go first," I manage to say, cutting off whatever she was about to add.

Deep breath, Gabriella. If you don't share how you feel, how can you expect her to know? Right? Right.

I turn back to her after my internal pep talk ends.

"This is going to be extremely selfish and I'm going to only talk about myself, but I have to tell you how I feel or I'm worried I may never be able to get it out. Not communicating properly was our initial issue and I don't want to make that mistake again, so I hope you understand."

Jenna's face softens and she reaches out to grab my hand.

"Of course I understand, you can tell me anything."

Deep breath.

"Well, I obviously don't want you to leave. Selfishly, I know going to New York is the best career move for you but I don't want you to go. I'm so proud of you, though... My Jenna on Broadway. That's amazing."

I feel myself choke up and Jenna reaches out to wipe away the tear that managed to slip out.

"I'm horribly upset that you have to leave but so proud of you. I can't ask you to stay and I won't but I'm filled with an incredible emptiness when I think about losing you."

"Oh, Gabs." She pulls me into a hug. "You're not losing me... Haven't you heard of a long-distance relationship? Besides, it's not forever. You can come visit me. You work in tech, so don't you make a lot of money and have amazing vacation time?"

I smile. "Stop trying to out-logic me. I would've gotten there eventually... Maybe."

"I'm sure you would have, darling. For the record, those are all very valid concerns. I don't want to lose you either. I'm putting on a brave face right now, but I was terrified when I got the call that I got the job. Of course, it's something that I've wanted for so long, maybe even my entire life. But you're also something I've wanted for so long."

"Really?" I sniffle in a vain attempt not to get snot on her sweater. We end our hug so I can look her in the face again.

"Yes. It was so hard leaving you the first time. I can't imagine doing it again."

"But you'll have to," I remind her.

"Yes, but this time you can actually come visit me. Since I'll be on land and in a fancy city, not in the middle of the ocean."

"That is a valid point..."

"Just because it'll be different, doesn't mean it won't work. You know there's always a handy invention called a cellphone. Have you heard of it?"

Jenna's tone is playful now and I can't resist joining in her teasing.

"Oh, is there? I haven't heard about it. What does it allow you to do?"

"Well, it lets you send messages and calls to your loved ones, anywhere across the world. It also has a handy camera so you can send pictures, videos, and do live calls."

"Wow!" I play up my shock at learning about such a useful device. "What kind of pictures and videos does one usually send?" I tease.

"Usually pictures of yourself or a cool attraction or landscape. Sometimes, people send some more salacious pictures."

"Salacious?"

"You know... A piece of ass here, a boob or two there."

I laugh.

"Well, we could do it, y'know," Jenna says now, more seriously.

"Do what? Send pictures?"

"Sure, you've never sent a nude before?"

I feel my face redden involuntarily, whether from embarrassment about being inexperienced in this realm or from the thought of receiving and storing a picture of Jenna on my phone.

"No, I haven't," I eventually admit.

"Oh my god, we have to take one now." Jenna leaps off the couch and holds out her hand for me to take.

"N-now? As in, right now?" Against my better judgment, I accept her outstretched hand and she leads me to her now-familiar bedroom.

"Yes, immediately. I will combust if I don't have a picture of you—your first picture—tonight," she practically squeals.

She sits me down on the edge of the bed and runs back out of the room, presumably to grab her phone from where she left it earlier.

When she returns, I have to fight off my urge to lean into her infectious excitement.

"What about privacy?" Working in the tech industry and having to read and see so many cybersecurity leaks, it's definitely at the top of my mind.

"Phones let you create private folders now—it'll be locked and only visible in that folder."

She kneels in front of me.

"I won't make you do anything you don't want to, of course. But this would be good practice for later."

Staring at her warm expression, it's hard to resist and I try to be honest. She looks so excited, especially compared to the somber conversation we had earlier.

"I guess I'm fairly open to trying new things. But I'm nervous. I've never been good at taking pictures, even just regular ones, of myself. Not sure how to start with sexy ones..." I trail off. My therapist would be extra proud of me tonight; openly sharing my feelings of inadequacy more than once and honestly.

"That's okay, I'll take them for you. Well, for me. These pictures are only for me," Jenna clarifies.

"Of course, I wouldn't want them to be for anyone else. Just for you." I smile at that, feeling more comfortable about it.

Jenna lowers herself to the ground in front of me, resting on her knees. She leans up to kiss me and I let her, enjoying the hungry way she directs the kiss. The sensation is familiar and welcome, and I love the feeling of letting her take control.

After a few minutes, she breaks away to look up at me again.

"I'll never get tired of that, but for now, shirt off."

I obey her wish and revel in her reaction. In the midst of tonight's conversation, I had almost forgotten again that I'm wearing her gift. Her reaction to it is worth it. She's looking at me as if I'm the last cake in the store and she's been craving it for weeks.

She rises up to kiss me again and I welcome it. As she begins kissing my neck and jaw, I whisper, "Do you like it?"

"Mmm, I love it. So sexy... Seeing you wearing what I picked out for you." She pauses to glance back up at me and I shift backwards so she can climb onto the bed with me. I tug at her shirt, inviting her to remove it as well, but she swats my hand away.

"This is all about you," she says and moves away to grab her phone. "You look perfect like that, so hungry for me."

"It would help if I could see you, I think," I admit. "I'm still getting a little freaked out over this whole thing."

"Okay, baby, your wish is my command." Jenna strips off her shirt and bra, leaving me breathless in awe.

"I can see the appeal of photos, now, I think." I stare at her.

Jenna tugs at my hand, leading me to sit up again as she positions herself in front of me.

"I'm going to take a picture now, okay?"

"You can do whatever you want." The sight of her breasts continues to distract me and I absentmindedly reach lower into my pants to alleviate some of the pressure there.

I focus on Jenna as she aims her phone camera at me and she looks up from the phone to my face. Her expression mirrors the want I feel.

"What are you thinking about right now?" she asks in a low voice.

"You, looking at these pictures later."

"And what would I be doing when I look at them?"

"Touching yourself, thinking of me, this moment." I quicken my own touches, finding the image intoxicating.

Jenna moves to put her phone on her nightstand and I watch with satisfaction as she shifts in front of me.

She notes my smile. "Oh, don't you look happy..."

"Yep, you got what you needed and now it's my turn."

"Bold, aren't you?"

I laugh and choose to respond with a kiss that leaves her moaning when I attempt to reach for her neck. She gets the hint and reaches for the hand that's still working on my own pleasure. She tugs and I allow her to lick my finger as she raises my hand to meet her lips.

"Oh," I can only mutter. This image will also be seared into my brain, watching her taste me so eagerly.

Seeing my reaction, she smiles widely and reaches for my underwear. I eagerly assist, lifting my hips to allow her to pull them down to my thighs.

I nod, breathless, as she aims her gorgeous lips lower. Her tongue brings me to the edge and it doesn't take long for me to experience sweet release. I reward her with some tongue action of my own and we end up lying in her bed together, sated and pensive again.

Perhaps the pensive part is just me. As if sensing my earlier doubts creeping back in, Jenna turns to me. In this position, it gives me a clear view of her nipple and I give it a small lick.

"Don't you start again," she warns without any real bite.

"Well, it was right there." I giggle and shift upwards so I can face her at eye level as we stare at each other.

This pillow is so comfy. One of many things I'll miss, I suppose.

Jenna reaches for me and smooths out my eyebrows. "You just had amazing sex with your girlfriend, so why do you look so troubled?"

"Because said girlfriend is about to leave next month."

"It's a whole month away and it's not leaving, just...temporarily operating out of a different home base."

I laugh at that.

"I know, I know. I'm working on getting comfortable with the idea."

"Phone sex will help with that too," Jenna jokes. "We can practise, but another night, though. The roller coaster of emotions combined with the crouching is starting to get to me."

I rub Jenna's legs sympathetically, enjoying how close the move brings us together. Jenna hums happily in response and I leisurely kiss her neck and jaw as she closes her eyes.

Just as I debate moving my hand higher, she opens her eyes and grabs my arm, bringing my hand to her lips. She pecks my knuckles.

I could stay like this for hours.

"Me too," Jenna says and smiles. I blink, not realizing that was something I said out loud. "We'll have to schedule mandatory cuddle time like this for the next month. I need my fill before I leave."

"I'll have to check my phone calendar," I joke, snuggling closer against her. I hum happily as she proceeds to play with my hair.

CHAPTER SEVEN

I accompany Jenna to the airport, my presence entirely unnecessary, especially from a logical perspective, but even I can't persuade myself out of seeing her off. I try to remember that I'll see her in no time, that the small island airport services New York and Toronto daily but that doesn't help my heart. Holding her hand as we Uber to Pearson somehow feels like I'm in control of something.

The driver must sense the somber mood because the ride is full of pop music at a low volume, and I feel like I'd have to strain to hear it. He also avoids asking any questions, an unusual trait for drivers riding to the airport. I have to assume, though, as it's been a while since I've been on a trip.

I take a deep breath and turn to Jenna, automatically smiling when I find her gaze fixed on me.

She rubs my hand and pecks my cheek. "It'll be okay."

When we arrive, I lead Jenna inside to the Air Canada terminals where she uses her passport to print out an automated ticket and luggage tag. The customer service reps appear out of thin air to take her to the luggage deposit, and I tag along, feeling more like deadweight than a necessity.

Now the moment has arrived and we stand off to the side

ACT TWO

awkwardly as streams of people rush by to head to the security line. I can hear the airport workers demanding to see passports and boarding passes, and it's clear that this will be our farewell point.

"Well, let me give you a hug for the road." I give Jenna the longest hug I've ever had in my life.

I rub her back absentmindedly, as if soothing her. I try not to tear up but my eyes act as if of their own violation and Jenna looks more blurry than usual when she leans back to look at me.

"Oh gosh, don't cry," she says, wiping my cheeks.

"I had no intention of doing so. I've been practising what I'd say for the past week."

"Oh, really? Your eyes seemed to have missed the memo." She smiles as she teases me.

My heart aches as I take a deep breath, trying to recall the way I had it laid out. The words escape me in the moment and I aim for the short version.

"I'm too emotional to remember exactly what I wanted to say." I hiccup, my lungs backing me up. "But the gist is that I love you, I'll miss you, and please become super famous so you can upgrade from a tiny bedroom to a place that has enough space for a home office, so I can work from your new place in comfort."

Jenna laughs and leans in for a sloppy kiss, made worse by the tears that are still more or less running down my face.

"I love you too, darling. I can't believe you were the one to say it first."

"I know, I've come a long way," I joke as I break away to scour my purse for a packet of tissues that I swore I threw in there yesterday. Mission achieved, I dab at my eyes and blow my nose in a very unsexy way.

"I'll text you when I land," Jenna says, leaning in for one final kiss. "But no promises on the successful thing. If anything, it should be your job in tech that carries us both."

I laugh and give her one last peck. I know if I say anything else, that will only make it worse, so I watch as Jenna smiles and walks towards security. I try to hold back a second wave of tears as Jenna leaves with one final wave my way. I watch as she presents her boarding information to the staff and disappears behind the partition leading to security.

"Wow, that was sooo cute," a familiar voice chimes from behind me.

I turn in surprise to find Tyler holding a comically large box of tissues.

"Oh my god, I can't tell you anything," I whine as I lean into his arms.

"There, there, sweet angel. Tell me everything on the way to the train."

"Wow, no Uber?"

"Some of us don't make manager money, you heathen. At least I actually came." Tyler elbows me and I smile, feeling grateful that, even in the hard moments, I always have friends that are there for me.

"Enough about me, let's gossip about you for once..."

EPILOGUE

Six months later.

The crowd applauds as Jenna bows for the final time, and I join them with a few hollers of my own. I know the shaky video I'm recording of the curtain call will likely contain more of my screams than the crowd's so I send a silent apology to Jenna as I end the recording. I hurry to grab my jacket and purse, rushing out of the theatre towards the stage door. I did my research and scoped out its location earlier, remembering to leave as soon as I can, following the advice I read online.

When I arrive, there's already a bit of a crowd and I have to go up on tiptoe to peer over the faces to make sure no one has come out yet.

I clutch my playbill in hand and flip through it. As Jenna is not part of the original cast, I take out the sheet of paper that shows her understudy details and tuck it into my purse for safekeeping. Do understudies even come to stage doors? I assume if they're leads and frequent cast members, they do—I feel my palms sweating as I imagine my grand plan crashing and burning.

I scroll on my phone as I wait and nervously text the group chat I have with Leslie and Tyler. He reassures me that my ridiculous plan will likely work and asks me to get the people around me to film it for him. Leslie agrees as well, sending a gif of someone cheering. This whole thing is ridiculous enough to give me heart palpitations, so I'm not going to add to it by talking to strangers, I text back.

I can see him send through a bunch of annoyed expletives, but before I can respond, cheering from the front interrupts me. I look up to find the stage door open and the famous indie singer who's playing the male lead walking out to a rush of adoring fans. Another castmate follows behind him, someone I recognize as playing the best friend character. Finally, Jenna emerges to a few more cheers. I should be surprised but I'm not; she's fairly popular on TikTok and her videos have been gaining her some new fans and sweet sponsorships that allowed her to move out of her shoebox.

Not that I've seen her new place in person yet, but what I've seen via FaceTime is pretty nice.

The crowd parts a little as people at the front of the line walk away, starstruck and chattering. As the crowd pulls me closer to the doors, I can hear the people in front of me complimenting the cast.

"You were so good, Brodie."

"How do you find the time to practise between this and Quixotic?"

"Seriously, Jenna, you were so amazing!"

That last line should be mine and it takes a great deal of effort for me not to accidentally elbow the person in front of me. I mutter a generic, "Amazing show!!" to Jenna's castmates and nervously wait as she gets closer. She's close enough now that I can see her taking a selfie with the person in front of me, and I can spot it in her eyes when she recognizes me. She hurries the fan off and I step forwards.

"I'm dreaming, right?" She blinks as I reach out towards her with my playbill.

"Nope... Hi," I settle for. I watch as she nervously signs the playbill, glancing between me and the paper.

"You did amazing, I recorded your bow. I don't know if I'm allowed to do that," I admit.

When Jenna looks back at me, there are tears in her eyes.

"Oh, baby," I say.

I want to reach over and brush back her tears, but with the way her stage manager is eyeing me, I doubt that would fly.

"I'll text you later," Jenna finally says as the crowd pushes me along.

I'm surprised by the reaction but I walk away and head over to the $1 pizza place to wait. As I walk, I glance back down at the playbill Jenna has signed. It takes me a while to decipher the words written across the loud poster.

MY HEART. THANK YOU.

Slightly reassured, I finish off a slice of pizza and begin to walk back towards the theatre when my phone buzzes with a call.

"Where are you?" Jenna's voice sounds hurried.

I look around and move to the side of the street. I name the bakery that I happen to be standing next to and am immediately told not to move, which is fine by me as I was getting tired of walking around.

Eight torturous minutes later, I see Jenna's unmistakeable pink beanie flying towards me. As she gets closer, I spread my arms wide as she launches herself into them.

"Hi." Her voice is muffled from where she has her head buried in my shoulder.

"Hi." I squeeze her for good measure.

"Sorry about earlier. I was so overwhelmed, seeing you. How did you get here so quickly?"

"Well, working in tech does have its perks," I say back.

"Thank you, thank you," Jenna says in between small pecks.

At the last peck, I deepen the kiss, showing her exactly how much I've missed her.

"Please tell me you have tomorrow off," I say as we finally break apart, to more than one wolf whistle from passersby.

Jenna nods and grabs my arm, tugging me towards the street. She hails a cab (*was that action always so sexy?*) and I watch in wonder as she tells the driver where to go.

"Wow, only a few months here and you already fit right in."

When we arrive, it's a short elevator ride to her new apartment.

I notice the flowers I had delivered waiting at the front of her door and my heartbeat quickens as I remember the last bit of the surprise.

Jenna exclaims as she notices them and she picks them up to smell.

"Wow, who could these be from?" she asks, her tone suggesting she knows exactly who they're from.

"Let's go inside and find a vase to put them in," I suggest helpfully.

She laughs and unlocks the door. She deposits the flowers on the counter to the left of the entrance and I take my time taking off my shoes and jacket. My pants pocket stays firmly closed and I breathe a sigh of relief.

Jenna returns to put her jacket away and I go back towards the flowers, rooting around in the cupboards for a pair of scissors to open the packaging.

I grab the envelope attached to the front and set it down gently.

Jenna returns to the kitchen and I stop in my tracks, admiring her properly for the first time in months.

"Wow, I've missed you," I whisper, temporarily forgetting about my plan.

"I've missed you too," she says, cornering me against the counter.

A passionate kiss leads to some pants grabbing and that snaps me out of my daze.

ACT TWO

"Hold on," I say as Jenna reaches for the front button of my jeans.

"Read this first." I lean past her to grab the envelope I discarded earlier.

"That can be done later, let's finish catching up first."

"It's important to me." I laugh as her neck kisses turn ticklish.

"Okay, okay." She breaks away and steps back. Grabbing the envelope from my hands, she tears it open. "Baby, I'm so proud of you," she starts reading aloud. "I hope you don't mind me disturbing your day—never," she interrupts herself. "Please visit me whenever you want," she punctuates her statement with a kiss.

"I'd be happy to, now keep reading."

"Bossy," she teases but goes back to it. She doesn't read the rest out loud but stops as she gets to the end. Her distracted seconds have allowed me to finally grab the ring from my pocket.

"It's not much but I hope it shows how serious I am about you," I say as I open the velvet box.

I'd kneel on the floor but this kitchen is cramped (this is NYC, after all) and I'm thankful I can see her reaction up close.

Jenna blinks slowly, looking between the note and me.

"This is actually happening, like, actually?"

"Yes... Now, will you give me an answer?"

"Of course I'll marry you!" She wraps me up in a hug and I lavish her neck, her cheek, her mouth with kisses. "I'm speechless. I didn't think this is where my day was going to go," she continues as she returns my kisses with some of her own and I welcome the break from smiling.

"Oh my god, now I can finally relax. I swear, I've been sweating off all my makeup in nervousness," I admit.

"Well, you can do more relaxing now that you're here. Would you like a tour? Perhaps the bedroom?"

Jenna grabs my hand and drags me into the depths of the apartment.

"Sure, let's start there."

"Good, because I have a lot planned for us. You'll be wanting an encore after I'm done with you."

"I can hardly wait."

THE END

ROOM FOR TWO

And they were roommates...

Stephanie Richards is not interested in dating, not interested in dealing with the awkward phase of meeting someone new. And if she sometimes finds herself dreaming about her best friend, Beatrice Cohen, that's her business.

But when Beatrice needs a place to stay, Steph finds herself closer to her unrequited crush than ever before. As Bea and Steph spend more time together, Steph starts to realize that perhaps her feelings aren't quite as unrequited as she thought.

Will their new roommate arrangement end in disaster or newfound love?

CHAPTER ONE

It's cheesy, but I love the CN Tower. Most people, though, like my best friend Bea, do not.

"Remind me, why are we here again, Steph?" she asks nervously as we wait in line to enter.

"Because my company is rewarding me for five years of hard work by sponsoring a dinner here tonight with anyone I want."

The last part is a bit of a stretch. My boss specifically told me I should impress a date here, but as dating prospects are slim and I much prefer Bea's company, I didn't take the suggestion seriously.

"Well, next time, tell them to choose someplace that doesn't require entering this death trap, please and thank you."

"Death trap? Millions of tourists come here every year without any issue. I've never heard of someone meeting their demise here."

Bea laughs. "Meeting their demise seems a bit dramatic."

"Compared to death trap, it seems pretty light," I tease back, the words having no bite to them.

We're called to present our tickets and I share the restaurant reservation information. They let us up with no problem.

As we queue for the elevator, Bea's apprehension returns.

"You've been here before, right? The elevator works fine?"

"Yes, I've been here before, as a kid. I've always wanted to come back. The view is pretty nice."

"Okay, I'll do my best to believe you..."

The line moves forwards and we follow the crowd silently. My silence is more due to the fact that my mind always relaxes when I'm around Bea, and the excitement of having a fancy (free!) meal is getting to me. Based on the look of her face, her excitement is probably the terrified kind.

"So, how was your day?" I ask, trying to ease her nervousness.

That at least makes her smile.

"It was good. I was able to catch up on some of the inventory records and my coffee crush came in."

Ugh.

"How exciting! What did they order this time?" I do my best to sound pleased for her.

"Just an iced oat milk latte like last time. But they complimented the window display," she answers dreamily.

Bea is the manager of a really cool bookstore and café, appropriately named Love A Latte Books, and she's in charge of most of the inventory and logistics. She occasionally takes on some of the café operations during breaks or lulls. The store mainly needs staff during the mornings, so the afternoon is usually quiet for the café and Bea tends to be able to handle it all on her own. This allows her to flirt with the really interesting folks who have the time to be out at 3pm on a random Wednesday for a coffee.

I try not to let my annoyance show.

"That sounds nice. Did you tell them you designed that amazing display?"

"Of course." She smiles proudly. "The least I can do after working so hard to make sure all the book covers are the exact same shade of purple is brag about it."

I hum in affirmation as she continues to describe the cutie's exact hair colour, amazing wardrobe, and appropriate book-themed tote. Finally, we arrive to the front of the line and it doesn't take long for us to get into the elevator.

Bea immediately walks to the back corner, as far away from the windows as possible, and I follow her.

"Here, I'll block you from the view," I offer, facing her instead of the attendant at the front, who is proceeding to do a headcount.

Too quickly, the doors close and we begin the ascent. I tune out the attendant as I focus on blocking Bea's view of the windows.

When was the last time I looked at her face in such detail? I'd forgotten how pretty the freckles lining her face are, and my heartbeat quickens from how close we are, not from the high-speed elevator.

Less than an excruciating minute later, the door opens and we all file out. I exhale shakily as the crowd disperses and we find ourselves on the main observation deck.

"Scary, right?" Bea asks, visibly trying to calm herself.

I nod, not wanting to elaborate, and start heading towards the 360 Restaurant.

After a few minutes confirming our reservation under my manager's details, we're seated at a small table closest to the large windows. The view outside is beautiful, the sunset mirroring off the tall buildings creating a beautiful orange glow.

I take a few pics and then offer to take one for Bea, telling her how amazingly the view complements her outfit and the light shade of pink that hasn't quite faded from the ends of her hair when she dyed it at the end of winter. She nods, and after a few pretty pictures, I show her my phone to ask whether she likes them or not. If there's one thing I've learned from my photogenic sister, it's that you need to confirm the person is happy with the photos as you're taking them, and not after when the moment has passed. I've been on the receiving end of too many complaints that photos are not quite right days later.

"Oh, I love these! Can you please send them to me? I'll have to add some to my online dating profile."

"Of course! Those are great pictures," I agree, while ignoring the internal stab at her words. What stab? *Bea is your friend, you nincompoop,* I scold myself.

Before I can give the wayward feeling any more thought, the server arrives to take our drink order. I order a fruity mocktail but encourage Bea to order an alcoholic drink if she'd like. I'd get one for myself but it tends to put me to sleep, and I much prefer being awake for expensive dinners.

In addition to our drinks, the waiter appears with two glasses of Prosecco.

"So, what are we celebrating tonight, ladies? An anniversary?"

I hope that the blush I feel coming on stays hidden beneath my makeup.

I'm about to correct them when Bea speaks up. "Yes, how did you guess? It's our second year together, right, baby?" She reaches over and grabs my hand for emphasis.

"How wonderful! I'll give you some time to peruse the fixed prix menu and you can let me know when you're ready to make your selections."

Bea nods enthusiastically and I manage a small smile in agreement.

"You don't have to do this," I say, trying to sound calm. We've held hands before, I think. . . but why does this feel so different?

"Why not? If it'll help us get the best treatment, I'm always happy to put on a show."

I laugh despite my sudden nervousness and extract my hand from hers as calmly as possible. Maybe the special treatment from the restaurant is something my manager requested when they made the booking. I'll have to ask Cheri when I get to work tomorrow.

"So, besides seeing your work crush, what else has been going on lately?" I ask, trying to steer the conversation in a different direction.

Thankfully, this was the right question because Bea starts excitedly telling me about the local author visiting next month and about how thrilled she is to see them. I haven't read anything for pleasure in who knows how long but it sounds like an interesting book and I make an effort to remember it for later.

When the server returns to ask for our orders, Bea takes the lead, surprising me by remembering what I told her I wanted to get. Her taking charge makes me think about what other scenarios she gets bossy in, and I have to mentally close that rabbit hole before I fall down it.

The rest of the meal passes by fairly smoothly, and at the end, I charge it to the company card Cheri handed me earlier.

As we wait in line to take the elevator down, Bea reaches out to take my arm.

"I'm nervous. I don't know if I can do that death contraption again."

I smile, resisting the urge to tease her about the fact that she just sat down in front of a wide window overlooking the view without any issues for the past hour and a half.

"Do you want to hold my hand?" I offer, holding it out. She accepts it easily.

This is not the first time we've held hands, but like many firsts this evening, it feels a bit special. Maybe the relaxed atmosphere of the evening is letting my mind wander to places I usually try to keep closed.

The elevator ride itself is smooth and Bea keeps her eyes closed, visibly straining to control her breathing. When we get back to ground level, I guide her out of the elevator and we follow the crowd to the gift shop.

She still seems shaken, and I squeeze her hand once for comfort.

"C'mon, let's look through the gift shop and see if there are any items worth adding to Love A Latte Books."

Bea smiles wide at that. "You are so smart."

"I know, it's a gift," I say in a tortured tone and chuckle as she rolls her eyes and walks away.

As she browses the store with an eagerness far too adorable, I can't help but think, *If I was so smart, I'd stop thinking about you like this.*

CHAPTER TWO

"Good morning, MVP," Cheri says to me from behind the reception desk as I walk into the office the next day.

"Morning. How was your evening?" I ask with a genuine smile. Today's Thursday, which means tomorrow is a work-from-home day and I can hardly wait. Thursdays feel like Friday-lite, and with yesterday's intense energy, I need all the relaxation I can get.

"Mine was great! Just had enough time to see Cody in the talent show at school. He sang a musical number from Hamilton —the funny one."

Cody is Cheri's adorable son. I've seen clips from his rehearsals, and while he isn't exactly a musical genius, he made up for it with a genuine enthusiasm that only a 10-year-old could have.

"That sounds lovely." I stand in front of the desk now, grabbing the mug of tea Cheri already has ready for me.

"You're the best," I say gratefully. People can make fun of me all they want, but Earl Grey is a classic and it's the perfect remedy for all ills, including having to work in the office rather than on the couch.

"How was your night?" Cheri asks, deliberately tearing her

eyes away from her computer screen to look at me. I know it's a serious question when she ignores the computer ping of a new email in the background.

"It was good. Please send my thanks to Jeff again for the meal."

"How was the VIP package?" she asks with a knowing smile.

"It was good. We had a nice time."

Cheri groans in frustration. "C'mon, you have to give me more than that. We splurged on the best package for you and a date. So how was the date??"

I laugh, waving away her antics. "It wasn't a date. I just took my best friend."

"Oh."

Cheri seems disappointed by this news and it's not hard to imagine why. As my work mom (her words), she has taken it upon herself to see me happily with someone. It's almost sweet how much she's invested.

"I'm sure if I took someone I was dating, it would've been very romantic," I say in an attempt to cheer her up. "Thank you for all the effort you're putting in. When I have something to share, you'll be the first to know."

Cheri smiles and starts to reply when the phone rings.

"Parker and Associates, how can I help?" she answers, smiling apologetically at me.

I take another sip of my tea while I wait for her to wrap up the call.

"One moment, please," she says into the line, pressing the hold button and looking back at me. "We have to cut our chat short. There's a candidate on the line for you about their interview tomorrow," she tells me.

I nod and tell her to forward the call to my office. Sitting down in the small corner unit, I listen to the candidate and reassure them that they'll do great tomorrow in the interview. As part of a company that specializes in recruitment of executive roles on behalf of larger organizations, most of my day is spent working on documents for new job postings, interviewing potential job candidates, and attending and facilitating interviews.

The rest of the workday flies by, as I spend time looking for candidates for another open role and read over some open calls from companies looking for outside help with their hiring processes for new CEOs. I'll have to have my assistants help me with crafting our submissions for consideration.

Cheri and I never end up finishing our chat and I spend lunch with Jeff Parker (of the aforementioned Parker & Associates, of course) in the break room. By the time I head home, I'm grateful that we can hopefully table the conversation for the next little bit. It's been far too long since I've dated, or tried to think about dating. Work has been keeping me busy and I've been happy enough couch-rotting at the end of the workday and watching the latest reality show. The weekends are typically reserved for visiting my sister who relocated to the suburbs with her husband last year. While it's geographically close, anyone who lives in the Greater Toronto Area knows that visiting the family up north outside the city proper requires a whole weekend with how much time it takes to commute.

When I get home, I text my sister a view of yesterday's dinner with an update about it. I can regale her with the whole story on the weekend (I find it's always best to come loaded with one story for the dinner table) but I know she appreciates the live updates. She told me once that she misses our closeness, now that we're no longer roommates, and the way we would talk about every little thing. I try to make sure she feels that sentiment across text, and our conversation chain usually reads like one long brain dump.

I'm about to reply to her questions and update when a call from Bea comes through. *That's odd.* We only call each other in emergencies, and it's been a while since anything deemed that serious was discussed.

"Hey, everything okay?" I say right away.

"Actually, no." Bea's laugh turns into a sniffle. *Oh God.*

"What happened? I'll come get you," I say immediately, not giving her a chance to elaborate.

"It's okay, let me explain." She takes a deep breath. "Our washroom had a small drip coming from the ceiling into the bathtub and the building finally investigated it today. Of course, the pipes from the toilet above need a complete overhaul so our only washroom will be a renovation zone for the next week, they say. . . But we all know how Toronto repairs work, so it'll probably be more like a month." Bea groans and I can hear a flop in the background; likely a defeatist fling onto her bed.

"What am I going to do without a washroom for the next month?" I hear a sniffle again.

"Come stay with me. You know my place isn't big but I have a foldout couch and my bed, as you say, is singularly too large for one person."

Bea laughs. "Are you sure? I can't ask that of you."

"I'm pretty sure this is in the best friend contract, section 12, line 18."

I can practically hear her smile. "That's right, I do remember reading that."

"Just pack a bag and I'll send an Uber to get you when you tell me you're ready."

"Wow, luxury," Bea jokes. Her tone turns serious. "Thank you so much, Steph. I don't know what I'd do without you."

"It's what friends are for," I respond without hesitation.

While Bea packs, I dig through the storage bin included in the sectional part of my couch for extra linens so I can set her up comfortably. I also pull out an extra pair of king-size bedsheets for my own bed, trying to remember the last time I washed the sheets. I don't think she'll want to share a bed with me —we haven't done that since we were on vacation a few years ago with some other mutual friends—but you never know.

I'm deep into vacuuming when a text ping interrupts my playlist and I order Bea an Uber to my place. Despite being only 2km away, it will take 15 minutes for the car to get here—something that was definitely an adjustment when I first moved to Toronto. Despite the high rent and small living spaces, I still have an unhealthy love for this city that I haven't been able to shake since I first started university here. My friends tease me for it relentlessly but it comes in handy in moments like this. While some of my friends have already started the move back to suburbia, I've been holding on to this tiny apartment with its fixed rent for far too long, as has Bea with hers. Catch-ups with our other friends now take weeks to coordinate but they're worth it, and I know that the events of today will be the most pressing topic of conversation for a while, as they try to convince us to give up the city life.

A call from the building's intercom system interrupts my reverie and I quickly buzz Bea up, putting the vacuum away and straightening out the kettle on the kitchen island while I wait.

A minute passes and there's a faint knock at the door. I let Bea in.

She has a small carry on-sized suitcase and she pauses at the door to take off her shoes.

"Welcome to your new home," I say, as cheerfully as possible.

"Thank you for having me," she replies.

"Of course!" I pull her in for a light hug in our usual greeting, and she wraps tightly around me, taking a deep breath.

"It's okay," I say, rubbing her back, "Everything will be just fine."

She detaches herself and shakes out her arms.

"I know, I know." She takes another deep breath as if to steady herself. Seemingly determined, she claps her hands together.

"Okay, so what are we having for dinner?"

"Pizza?" I offer, knowing it's her favourite food and she is unlikely say no.

"You are a genius and I love you," she responds.

I laugh and grab her suitcase, leading her into the fray. My heart stutters at her words, and my brain forces me to ignore the phrase, knowing it was said with our usual friendly banter and nothing more.

It can't be more, I remind myself.

∼

The next day, I wake up groggy and disoriented and hear crashing coming from the kitchen. Alarmed, I stumble out of the room to find Bea looking sheepish as a plastic cup rolls towards my feet. I stop it with my right foot.

"All okay in here?" I ask, stifling a yawn.

"Yes, sorry. I was trying to get my favourite mug for a morning tea. Why is it all the way at the back of this cupboard and why do you not have anything other than Earl Grey?"

It's at the back of the cupboard because I know it's your favourite and I save it for you—but I don't say that.

"Sorry, I haven't used it in a while, and you know about my tea preferences. Do not slander the best tea."

I grab the cup from the floor and walk over to stand next to Bea. I drop the cup into the sink and reach to the back of the cupboard for her desired mug, my height giving me an easy advantage. Our hands brush as I hold it out to her.

"What kind of tea do you want? I'll pick some up on my lunch break."

Bea's eyes light up and I watch her do a mental ranking of all the tea flavours she can think of. I can almost read her mind in these moments and I can't help the smile on my face by the time she's finished her analysis.

"Something fruity? Maybe a peach tea," she finally decides.

"Done."

With nothing more to discuss, I suddenly realize I'm wearing my short nightdress, one that I normally don't let anyone see. I assumed I wouldn't be seeing Bea this morning before she went to work and decided to wear something more comfortable rather than appropriate. I blush as I head back to my room.

"See you later, have a good day at work," I call out as I close the door to my room.

"You too," Bea calls back.

As I flop back into bed, I hear the kettle ping on before I return to dreamland.

∼

It's 3pm on a Friday, which means that no work is actually being done. I've been staring at this email for the past three minutes, trying to decide whether this is a task for Future Steph or not. A jingle at the door interrupts my existential crisis.

"I'm home," Bea singsongs.

I look up from where I'm sprawled up on my couch, and gently place the laptop that was resting on my stomach on the floor. I sit up as she starts removing her shoes and walks towards the couch.

She plops down unceremoniously next to me.

"Hard at work or hardly working?"

"Hardy har har," I deadpan back.

She laughs earnestly.

"So, what are you doing for the rest of the day?" I ask.

"Nothing much. Want to watch a movie or something?"

"Sure. I was just going to start that new reality TV show about the C-list actors—"

"The one where they have to work in regular places? I'm dying to watch the one about Dana Shostein from *Aurora Skies* working at a bookstore."

"Yes, that one. Want to watch it together?"

We make a plan to watch the show together later that evening, once 5pm hits and I can officially be 'off the clock'. I move my workstation to my bedroom and let Bea relax on the couch in peace as she's claimed it as her living space for the next few weeks. When it was time to choose beds last night, she ignored my offer to let her share my king bed. I'm sure she'll cave once her back starts hurting from the stiffness of the couch (as someone who's accidentally fallen asleep there many nights only to have to creakily move towards their bedroom at 4am, I would know) so I didn't press the issue.

I make it back to the couch at around 5:30pm, extremely apologetic and explaining that my boss called me at 4:56pm so I had no choice but to keep working.

"Anyway, what are you doing?" I ask as I sit next to Bea.

She was staring at her phone rather seriously before I sat down, half-waving my apology away.

"Oh, I was studying this person's profile before our date tomorrow." She holds the phone out towards me.

I flip through the profile quickly, trying not to read too much into it.

"She seems nice," I say when I hand the phone back.

"Nice is the best you can come up with?" Bea laughs.

"Well, I don't know her," I try. "When's the date?"

"Dinner tomorrow, and I am not opposed to being taken out for a meal. In this economy? Nice lawyer lady can invite me out any time."

"Definitely." I hum in agreement.

"What about you? Any salacious weekend plans?"

"Nothing salacious ever happens to me, on the weekend or otherwise, so no. Just going to visit my sister. Should I load the show?" I offer in an attempt to change the subject away from my non-existent dating life.

Bea agrees and we settle into our usual antics when we watch something together; talking over each other, groaning when the actors inevitably do their normal person jobs wrong, and pausing at key dramatic moments in the show to give our predictions. We break for dinner and I put some chicken in the air fryer (no one can convince me that the air fryer isn't the best invention in the past few years) and the rest of the night ends peacefully, the only interruption being my brain stuck on what Bea was looking at on her phone.

CHAPTER THREE

"Sorry, I think we need to reschedule," my sister Melanie says over the phone. I'm about to ask why when she sneezes, pre-empting my question. "As you can hear, we're all under the weather right now. I think Liam caught something at school."

"That's fair, no problem. I hope you all get better soon. Do you need me to send up soup or something?"

"Don't worry, Mom already took care of it. I can tell you've been ignoring the family group chat because we discussed this all yesterday. What were you up to?"

"Nothing, really, Bea is staying with me for a little bit because her apartment is dealing with some flooding issues so we were just watching TV until she passed out on the couch."

"Oh, that's nice. Will your place be okay for the two of you? Isn't your apartment smaller than a shoe box?"

I snort.

"Okay, Miss Suburbia, I seem to remember you used to live in an even smaller apartment with Chris before you bought that fancy house."

She laughs but it turns into a cough after a few seconds.

"I'll let you go. You should rest," I say definitively, knowing we could talk on the phone for hours.

"Thanks, I'll text you later," she says before hanging up.

With nothing to do for the rest of the day, I decide to head out to the living room to see what Bea is up to. Not sure exactly how to go about everything, I've been trying to give Bea her space in the living room while I hole up in my room. Perhaps I don't need to be so cautious but I know how much she values her alone time and I don't want to be hovering over her shoulder at every moment. After lunch, she fell asleep on the couch (she also loves her naps) and I wanted to make sure to leave her alone, so I killed some time looking up some new crochet designs. I haven't done it in years but I think I need something to keep me busy. The crochet game has changed since I've been in it, and the number of awesome online tutorials and cool patterns on Etsy is unreal.

I carefully open my bedroom door, poking my head out.

No sign of life.

I step out into the room, noting that the blanket and sheets on the couch have been neatly folded and placed on the corner of the ottoman.

I head to the washroom, where I find a disaster zone; makeup products littering the counter and an empty cloth makeup bag lying on the floor.

I snort and walk away, grabbing my phone from the charger on my nightstand where I left it after my call with Mel.

I have an unread text from Bea from 17 minutes ago.

> Sorry the washroom is a mess, I overslept from my nap.

Ah, that explains it.

> No worries, enjoy your night out!

Well... now what? I could spend the evening feeling sorry for myself (which I do more often than I care to admit these days) or I can put on some TV and try out one of those new crochet patterns I saw online.

In a feat of motivation rare for me on weekends, I manage to dig my crochet materials out of my closet and get started on a stuffed narwhal pattern for Liam. He's going to love it and I will win Aunt of The Year in a competition that I play against no one.

Dinner passes by uneventfully, with a sugary bowl of cereal for comfort and I text Mel to check in while I eat. My text to Bea has gone unread—we insist on turning on read receipts for each other, one of few people I leave the setting on for—and I try not to think too hard about it. If I was on a date (internal scoffing at the very notion aside), I wouldn't want to be on my phone.

When I start yawning in front of the TV later that night, I decide to head to my room and turn in. Despite thoughts about Bea's date sneaking into my consciousness every so often, I manage to fall asleep quite easily until I'm woken by my bedroom door creaking open.

"Oh, you're here," Bea says as I groggily prop myself up to see what's going on.

"Yes, Mel's family all has a cold so she cancelled earlier," I reply, sitting up properly this time. I switch my bedside lamp on.

"You don't have to get up. Sorry, you were right. I was getting tired of the couch. . ." She trails off and turns away but I hear the weakness in her voice. A sniffle from the living room confirms my suspicions.

I stand, hurrying to the living room. She's sitting on the couch in the dark, makeup slightly smudged and an unglazed look to her eyes.

"Come on, tell me about it. I can't leave you like this." I stand in front of her, holding my hand out.

She looks up at me and I can see the hurt in her eyes. I should've studied the profile she showed me more carefully so I can track down who did this to her and kick them.

"Okay." She accepts my outstretched hand, and I lead her back to my room, my normal rules about not wearing outdoor clothes in the bed forgotten as she sits next to me.

"What happened?" I ask softly.

Bea sighs and shifts lower from where we're both leaning on the headboard.

"It was going well; it was fun, even. We had a drink and were just sharing stories over really annoying customers, or clients, in her case. And then, of course, we get to the topic of housing and how annoying it is living in this city, when she starts telling me about her roommates, or at least people I assumed were her roommates."

"They weren't?"

"No, of course not. They were her partners, who all sounded amazing and great." Bea groans. "She was nice but that's not the situation I expected, and of course, I was a little annoyed because it wasn't listed anywhere on her profile! We had a great conversation, but it just feels like I was misled about what the situation would be."

"That's tricky, I'm sorry," I earnestly say.

"It's just. . . when will it be my turn? I'm starting to feel like I won't be able to find anyone to share my life with. I don't think I have lofty goals, and I'm p-pretty hot, right?"

She stumbles through her words a little as she starts crying again, tears sliding down her face. I turn towards her and wipe her tears away with my left hand, the wipe turning more into a caress of her face.

"You're extremely hot," I say, still wiping at the tears that slowly fall. The tears end but I keep my hand on her cheek, slowly rubbing her chin.

"Even when I'm crying?" she asks, a hiccup punctuating the question.

I smile softly.

"Even then," I admit, my eyes darting down to her lips.

Were they always so enticing? I should stop, back away and turn the conversation to a more friendly one but my body acts as if on its own accord. I can't bring myself to stop caressing her cheek and my thumb moves to her lips. I lightly bring my hand to her lower lip and chin.

I move closer, but I stop myself an inch from her face. I search her eyes for an answer to the question I'm too afraid to ask, and she looks back at me. I can name most expressions I've seen on her face but this is a new one; probably for us both.

She seems to have read my face correctly because she leans in slowly, and before I know it, we're kissing. It starts slow, warm, and quickly turns a little frantic when I realize I'm finally doing what I've dreamed about for longer than I care to admit. She kisses me back with a similar amount of enthusiasm and I try not to read too much into it.

I lean back for a bit of a break, breathing deeply. Bea looks at me with wide eyes, as if I've suddenly turned into a stranger. A small frown appears on her face as I smile.

"This wasn't a pity kiss, right?" she asks, now burying her face in her hands. "Oh God, did I just ruin everything?"

I move closer to her, lightly pulling her hands away from her face so she's forced to look at me.

"No, it wasn't," I answer, giving her a light peck on the lips for emphasis.

I pull her hands away from her face and down to rest at her sides, then kiss her on the neck, slowly moving up towards her jaw so I can whisper into her ear. If I say the words aloud, maybe I'll snap out of whatever spell I'm in, retreat from the feelings that I'm finally letting show.

"Let me show you how much I want this."

"Oh," she sighs as I start kissing in reverse, working my way down from her jaw to her clavicle. The bottom of her dress rides up as I slowly move my right hand up her thigh.

As I reach for the waistband of her cotton underwear, I look at her face. A small nod is all I need to pull down the fabric and press small kisses along her legs, working my way up.

It's been a while since I've gone down on a woman but I must be doing something right as Bea tugs on my hair as I continue. Small moans rise from her and the sound encourages me; I pick up the pace. I feel her tense and I slow down, my tongue moving slower as I try to support her orgasm.

She cries out, a sound I haven't heard from her before, and I kiss her thighs when I'm done, taking my time before I have to leave whatever dream I'm in and face reality.

Her expression is warm when I finally bring myself to face her and my own heat responds, begging for attention.

"When did you learn to do that, Steph?" she asks, moving closer so she can loop her arms around my neck.

"There's a few things you don't know about me," I answer, aiming for mysterious.

"Well, should I find out?" She leans in to kiss me, and before I know it, I'm lying on my back with her straddling me.

My kisses turn frenetic, and I almost don't know where to put my hands; on her shoulders, down her arms, up across her stomach?

She breaks away from my lips, now working her way down my jaw.

"You don't have to—" I start to say when a moan of my own interrupts me.

She giggles, kissing me on the lips again.

"Maybe just a little touch then," she says, lowering her hand into my pyjama bottoms.

It doesn't take long for me to turn into a quivering mess, any logical thought abandoned as I chase her hand and cry out her name as she matches my pace.

Afterwards, she kisses me again as I grab her hand to wipe on my pyjama shirt.

"Don't want your dress to get dirty," I explain when she raises an eyebrow at me.

Her eyes search mine for a moment and the unfamiliarity of the situation hits me. *Oh God, where do we go from here?* I don't know the answer to the question, and I'm scared to find out what she's thinking. This can't have been as serious to her as it was to me, and I don't want to scare her off.

"Let's go to sleep," I finally say and she takes the hint to roll off me. I crawl back to my usual sleep spot on the bed and hold out an arm for her, an open cuddle invitation.

She hesitates for a moment but crawls in next to me, lifting the covers over us both.

"Thank you," she finally says and I stay silent, worried an answer will give me away. So I just kiss her on the temple and pull her closer, relishing her familiar warmth against me.

∼

I wake up in an empty bed. It seems that whatever part of my brain has kept my feelings for Bea closed off has decided to unleash in full force and I find myself missing her. I ignore the feeling and crawl over to the side of the bed that has my nightstand, reaching for my phone. A single unread text from Bea shows on the lock screen.

> Had an early shift today, will see you later!

The text reveals nothing. What if she's starting to regret what happened last night? The thought wakes me up and I go towards the washroom, taking a quick cold shower to rationalize the events of yesterday and wash up.

By the time I've eaten breakfast and done my typical weekly chore of laundry, I've convinced myself that she is regretting this whole thing and will want to move back out immediately.

Deep breaths. I call the only person I can think of to help.

"Everything okay?" Cheri answers after the first ring.

"Sorry to bother you on the weekend. Do you have a few minutes? I'm kinda going through it right now."

"Of course, anything for you." Her own sentence is interrupted by a high-pitched scream in the background and I hear her voice tell a child to calm down. I hear some shuffling, then the distinct sound of a door closing.

A deep sigh later, and she's back.

"Sorry about that, honey, you know how it is. So, what can I do for you?"

I laugh. "Never a dull moment at your house, right?"

"Never," she confirms.

"Well, so you know how I mentioned yesterday that Bea is staying with me for a little bit—"

"The best friend, the one you took to dinner, right?" she interrupts to confirm.

"Right, that one. Anyway, I couldn't go to Mel's yesterday because everyone is sick—"

"Oh, I hope she gets better soon," she interrupts again.

"Yes, yes, I'll tell her. Anyway, I was home and Bea came home from her date and came to my room—"

"Wow, dating in Toronto! Someone I know could take a page out of her book," she interrupts again.

"Cheri, I love you but if you don't let me finish this story in one go. . ."

"Sorry, sorry, I just get so excited. Go ahead," she says after we both laugh at my non-threat.

"Anyway, one thing led to another and there may or may not have been a make-out session last night. Well, maybe more than making out. . ."

An unnaturally long pause follows. I'm about to ask whether everything is okay when she chimes in, "Can I speak now?"

"Yes, that was it."

I laugh as she gives a high-pitched scream.

"Oh my god, when I was trying to manifest a suitable partner for you, I didn't think it would take effect right away."

"Woah, woah, we're not at partner stage yet. Technically, we haven't even left the friend stage. That's why I'm calling. What do I do?"

"Well, that depends," she says and then hums as she mulls it over. "What do you want to do?"

"I don't know. I'm not used to this, being vulnerable. I prefer to just not say anything. It's easier to just keep living my life as I normally do."

"And where is that getting you? Here on the phone with me, freaking out because you don't know how to process your feelings."

"Well, it's not that I don't know my feelings, I'm just scared to share them. What if it doesn't work out and then I'm left truly alone?"

"You can't be so pessimistic; maybe it will work out. You can't be scared of the ending when there hasn't even been a start yet."

I sigh, trying to take her words to heart.

"Being vulnerable is scary! Can't I just stay closed off forever?"

"But then you lose out on so many wonderful things," Cheri says sweetly, and I can practically picture her staring at a picture of her family.

"Well, you lucked out on the life lottery with your wife and kids," I say honestly.

I can tell she's about to start scolding me again but the laundry beeps to announce its completion and I hurry to end the call, feigning urgency in the chore. While I could easily talk to Cheri more, and we have spent many times on the phone together for too long, the conversation was turning too pensive for my own good. I've done my best to avoid the thoughts that are now pinging around in my mind. *What if you can have it all? What if she regrets everything? What if you're really as undesirable as you think you are?*

I do a full-body shake, hoping that the physical movement will allow the thoughts to calm down. No such luck.

I wonder how Bea is doing. The thought appears and I decide this is the most sensible thought of the day. She must also be feeling something, even if it's just awkwardness, after yesterday. I hope her shift is going okay.

With nothing else to do other than stare at the now-spinning dryer, I decide that maybe I should go check on her. I haven't been to Love A Latte Books in a while and I want to try that lavender latte that Bea told me about recently.

Before I can talk myself out of it, I grab a cute tote bag and a long-forgotten book off the bookshelf in the living room (which was functioning more as décor rather than something with purpose) and I head out. My hair is a mess so I decide to add a baseball cap to my graphic T-shirt and jeans combo. My sneakers are mostly white (because I can only wear them on weekends, stupid corporate) and I am thankful that, all-in-all, I look pretty put together.

A 35-minute ride on the subway later, I'm standing in front of the bookstore's doors. I walk in past the display of books to the back where the store is bustling, full of activity. People seem to be either working (even on a Sunday!), reading, or chatting with friends and partners alike. I spot Bea back towards where the books are, cleaning up a display table. I quickly look away and push my baseball cap a bit lower. *Oh my god, what am I doing here?*

Not wanting to chicken out before I've even spoken to her, I decide to order the lavender latte. The barista is nice but I'm too distracted to try and make friendly chitchat, so I scroll on my phone as I wait for the drink.

Drink in hand, I walk back towards where the seating area is. Most of the tables are full and I decide I'm going to have to settle for sitting across from a couple that seems to be reading a non-fiction book together. I can't tell if I admire the dedication or if it just annoys me because of how cute it is.

"Is this seat taken?" I ask, pointing to the chair across from the taller of the two, a brunette with long hair tied up in a messy bun.

"Not at all." Her partner smiles, a petite blonde woman with a kind smile.

"Thanks, the café is busy today," I say, sliding in. I smile as the brunette raises an eyebrow at me. Message received.

I pull my book out of my tote bag and open it to a random page. My own thoughts distract me too much to allow me to concentrate, and after a few minutes of staring at the same page, I allow my concentration to shift towards the conversation across from me. It's not that I mean to eavesdrop but one perk of living in a city with so many interesting people is that there's no shortage of people-watching opportunities.

"I hope it works out for her," the blonde woman says.

"Me too, but we can't go inserting ourselves into everything, Jenna."

"Why not, Gabriella? She clearly needs someone to talk to, so we should invite her out with us tonight."

"We can't just adopt every single one of your fans."

"But she needs our help. It's a disaster waiting to happen and she can't even ask the one person she would normally talk to." Jenna, the blonde, sighs after saying this.

What the hell are they talking about? Curiousity almost makes me want to ask them but I'm interrupted by a hand on my shoulder. I turn to find Bea looking down at me, a mug in her hand and a slight smile on her face.

"Hey, didn't expect to see you here," she says. She places the cup, a store-branded mug and not a to-go cup like I bought earlier, in front of me.

"Figured you may want your usual Earl Grey."

"Thank you," I say sincerely.

"You in disguise today?" she teases, booping the front of my hat with her now-empty hand.

"Bad hair day," I laugh. "How's your shift going?"

"Great! I'm actually so excited to see you. I don't know if you recognize who you're sitting in front of!"

Bea looks towards the couple in front of me and she smiles widely at them. They glance my way again, clearly trying to read the situation better.

"Sorry, I don't think I do. . ." I say as apologetically as possible, which is not hard since I do feel guilty about eavesdropping on their conversation.

"That's Jenna Daniels, the Broadway star!! I've only sent you her TikToks a gazillion times. And her fiancée. . ." Bea trails off, looking apologetic at forgetting the brunette woman's name.

"Gabriella, and it's okay." She waves a hand as Bea clearly starts to try to apologize. "Jenna is the actual famous person, I'm just here to support her." She smiles at her fiancée and they share a look that is so sweet that it makes Bea sigh.

I take a sip of my drink to tamp down the annoyance, not wanting to think about it stemming from jealousy.

"You two are so cute. Jenna's video talking about your proposal didn't go viral for no reason. It was soooo cute."

"Oh yeah, that was wild," Gabriella says, eyes lighting up. "I can't believe she got to go on *Good Morning America* after that."

Jenna lightly swats Gabriella's arm.

"It wasn't because of that, it was to promote the show I was doing. The viral video was just an added bonus."

Gabriella nods in fake acquiescence and I take the moment to jump in.

"What show are you doing now, then?"

"Just rehearsing for the upcoming season. I'm still trying to get my bearings for the next show I'm in. It hasn't been announced yet so I don't want to say too much."

"That's so cool," Bea says breathlessly.

Never in my life have I been so relieved to learn that someone is engaged and it is this fact about the couple in front of me that keeps me calm. God, now that I've opened that door in my mind, it seems that any instinct to stop my wandering thoughts is gone.

"And how do you know Beatrice?" Gabriella asks me, smiling as she curls an arm around her fiancée.

"Oh, she's my best friend." The response comes out as second nature.

"Yes, Steph's letting me crash at her place because she's the nicest ever," Bea says in her usual way of describing me. This time, it sets off a flutter of butterflies. *I'm so gone.*

Jenna widens her eyes slightly but takes a sip of her drink as if to stop herself blurting out something.

"Oh, that does sound nice," Gabriella interjects.

Their reactions strike me as strange and a horrible thought occurs to me. *Did Bea tell them about us and that's what they were reacting to?!*

Jenna glances at me and then reaches into her bag to grab a pen. She beckons Bea closer with her hand and Bea complies, leaving me to go to their side of the table and I already miss her warmth.

Jenna reaches for Bea's arm and quickly writes down a number.

"Text me later, so we can talk about the thing you were telling us about earlier." Jenna glances at me as she says this, confirming my suspicions.

Great, now a celebrity knows more about my dating problems than I do.

Bea giggles and whispers something to her. I glance at Gabriella to find her staring at me, a cool smile on her face. I realize I should probably go back to my book.

Bea taps my shoulder again after a few minutes of whispered conversation. The number written on her arm seems to glare at me.

"I'm going to go help everyone get ready for closing in an hour. Want to stick around until then? We can go home together."

Go home together. The simple words sound too nice and I smile.

"Sure. I have this tea to finish anyway." I nod towards the large mug she placed in front of me earlier, now probably at the perfect drinking temperature.

"Great, see you then." Bea smiles and waves goodbye.

I watch her for a few more moments as she goes to talk with more customers. Regulars, I assume, by the way they respond to her and tease her about her lack of weekend plans.

I turn my head to glance back towards my book, catching Jenna's eye in the process.

"She's special," she says to me, as if in warning.

"I know," I say, trying to smile. Without anything else to say, I turn back to my book and try to get back to the page that I'm too distracted to focus on.

When the café closes, Jenna and Gabriella walk out, with Jenna stopping to give Bea a hug on her way out. Feeling awkward, I wait at the seat I've been occupying for the past hour. I managed to read two chapters, finding myself slowly getting lost in the author's writing. I was even successful in tuning out the lovebirds in front of me and that, in and of itself, is a win.

When the shop is finally empty, I walk over to the serving area with my mug.

"Where do you want this?" I ask the server who helped me earlier.

Now that I'm not trying to avoid anyone, I notice that they have a pin on their shirt that says 'Brodie (they/them)'. Their features are generally masculine and they have long brown hair that is the perfect amount of shaggy. I almost want to ask them for their haircare routine because my hair could never be that luscious.

I must be staring for too long because they turn away and clear their throat before turning back to me.

"I'll take it," they say, their voice surprising me in its huskiness.

"Thanks," I respond. Just as I decide to introduce myself, Bea appears and puts an arm around them.

"Is my bestie bothering you?" she asks them, ruffling their hair.

"No, they're not," they reply, rolling their eyes.

"You have to get used to it, Mx. Celebrity," Bea singsongs.

"Celebrity? I swear, how is everyone in here famous? I've never met so many famous people in my life," I say, leaning across the counter to join in the banter.

Brodie blushes, stepping out of Bea's hold.

"Not so much a celebrity anymore. I'm keeping it low key."

"Brodie is as humble as they are famous. You know Quixotic?"

"Oh, I think I've heard of them. Didn't they have that viral TikTok sound last year?"

"Well, here's their lead singer and songwriter. Brodie is a genius."

Brodie blushes even harder but turns away, taking the mug I was using to the sink at the other side of the back counter.

Bea moves closer to me, standing where Brodie was moments ago.

"It's a touchy subject for them," she tells me. "They're keeping a low profile here while they figure some things out."

I nod in understanding.

"That's why Jenna was here earlier, actually. The two of them met doing a Broadway production together last year."

"That's so cool. . . Even one tenth of your friends are cooler than all of me combined."

Bea laughs. "That's not true but I'm sure they would all appreciate it if they heard it."

"Sorry to interrupt, boss." Brodie appears again, standing nervously to Bea's right. "I'm all done cleaning up so I'm going to head out?"

"Good work today. I'll see you tomorrow." She smiles and waves bye as they head out.

And then we're alone. She smiles at me and I take a few seconds to stare back at her. Despite the long shift, she looks as beautiful as ever.

"Do you have a lot left to do?" I ask, finally remembering that we should probably have a conversation instead of staring at each other.

"Not really. I usually use this time to go around and check the book displays and shelves so I can sleep in tomorrow. It'll make everyone's morning tomorrow easier, and it's my favourite part about Sundays."

"You are so smart. . . Do you want any help?"

"Sure, follow me."

Bea leads me around the store, showing me the perfect way to line up the shelves (according to her many years of practice) and she leaves me to it with a squeeze of my shoulder. It takes much longer than I realize, and by the time I've finished the SFF section and most of the romances, my legs are burning from all the squatting, trying to reach the lower shelves.

As I work, I hear Bea bustle around near me and occasionally hear her murmurs to herself as she debates the merit of displaying each book. Taking a break to give my legs some rest, I watch her for a minute or two as she rearranges the table that's at the front of the store. As she pauses to stare at her work, she glances up at me and we make eye contact. I blush, feeling as if I got caught doing something I shouldn't have. After last night, as if I wasn't already drawn to her, it's as if she's caught me in her orbit and I can't find it in me to try and resist.

I turn back to my own work, and after twenty minutes, I'm done with the romance section and small selection of travel books.

I sigh and Bea appears at my side a moment later.

"You did it!" she says cheerfully.

"Yes, but just this side of the store. There's still those two sections over there," I groan, realizing that the right side of the store has been left untouched.

"It's okay, I texted Brodie to let them know they'll have to do the non-fiction section tomorrow before we open. I appreciate your help but you move really slowly," she teases.

"Wow, that's what I get after all my hard work?"

"I appreciate it anyway." She pats my arm in a 'there there' gesture and I resist the urge to reach out for her arm when she pulls away.

"So, are we going to talk about last night?"

She's asking me this now?! She's never been one to skirt around a conversation, and while I usually admire that trait, I don't think I'm quite ready for what I know will be inevitable.

"Your bluntness continues to amaze me." I break off in a slight laugh. "Sure," I agree.

"While last night was pretty great, I don't think it should

happen again. I don't want to take advantage of your kindness, and historically, it always gets a little messy when the lines between friendship are blurred."

"It wasn't kindness that made last night happen," I reply.

"Oh." She clears her throat, avoiding eye contact as a blush creeps across her cheeks.

As much as I would like to discuss it a little more, I realize I don't want to argue someone into being with me. If she doesn't want to cross that line, I have to respect her choice.

"But yes, crossing that line can make things tricky. We can pretend it didn't happen."

"I didn't say anything about pretending. We had a fun night and it can stay that way. Let's just not do a repeat."

I laugh and shake my head.

"You're ridiculous. I'm going to get my bag." I walk off towards the coffee bar where I left my tote bag and we proceed to head out towards the subway.

"Let's avoid mentioning this to the group chat," she says at a break in the conversation.

I agree, likely thinking the same thing she is. Our friend group has all been close since university where we first met and we experienced a fair share of awkwardness when Athena and CJ dated for about a year right after we finished school. They were really cute together, but when they broke up, CJ moved out of the city and Athena soon followed suit. It took a few months for us all to be able to even talk as a group, and while they're all right now, the post-breakup months were filled with drama; something that Bea and I never enjoyed. It was one of the many reasons we grew closer ourselves, beyond just being in the same friend group. Wanting a break from the drama had us spending many nights together, watching a new show or trying a new restaurant that went viral on social media.

On the subway, we manage to find seats and it makes me realize how tired I am. If I'm this exhausted, I can only imagine how Bea feels. She yawns, as if reading my mind.

"Why don't you nap a little? We have half an hour. I'll wake you up," I offer.

She smiles gratefully and closes her eyes, placing her head on my shoulder. I hug her closer, adjusting my posture so her head doesn't dig into my shoulder as strongly.

I hear her breathing even out and she's asleep within two minutes. I try not to sigh as I reflect on our conversation. It didn't go as I'd have liked it to but what did I even want to happen? While I've liked her for longer than I should've, she probably hasn't even given it a thought in the time I've known her. This isn't a movie and she isn't going to suddenly fall in love with me after we sleep together once. It sounds harsh even to my own ears and I try not to sigh again.

If she doesn't want a repeat of last night, that's fine. I'll go back to being the best friend that perhaps likes her a little too much and we can keep it at that.

CHAPTER FOUR

"So, how did yesterday go?" Cheri asks as soon as I walk into the Parker & Associates office the next day.

"Good morning to you too," I say, pausing at her desk to grab the Earl Grey she already has ready for me.

She always makes sure my Mondays are at least bearable and I need to cling to this routine to stay sane.

"Just fine. We talked about it and decided to keep that door closed. It's all good."

She raises an eyebrow and stares at me dubiously as I take a sip of my drink.

"This is the perfect temperature. Thank yooooou," I singsong as I walk away.

The phone rings in my office as soon as I step in and I pick it up, hoping it's the client I was waiting to call me back. Instead, it's Jeff, calling me with an update regarding a process we thought was finished.

"Looks like Pickleton wants even more changes to the job posting," he says, sighing, and I hear a keyboard clacking in the background.

"Sure. Send me an email and my team will get on it. I'm doing interviews all week, but I can probably find some time to squeeze it in."

"I will, but you're not going to like it. Don't say I didn't warn you."

When the email arrives, I can see why he warned me. The client suddenly wants to redo the entire marketing section about their organization, something my team already had to work way too hard on. It was stressful trying to find ways to pitch an organization that, to be honest, is like most other companies out there. This will keep me busy for the next little bit and I send a message to my lead writer saying that we'll need to talk.

"Well, there's nothing to do but get through it," I say, taking a sip of my Earl Grey for strength.

The rest of the week, aside from work, moves uneventfully. Work becomes a welcome distraction as the project we're working on continues to be capitalized by the demanding client and the number of revisions we have to do on documents that should've been simple is unreal. Juggling all that with interviewing, preparing candidates for interviews, and then evaluating those candidates exhausts all my mental capabilities. In a weird way, though, I'm grateful that work has been keeping me too busy to think about my personal life. By the time I finish on Friday, I'm ready to collapse on my bed and sleep for approximately two weeks. That seems like enough time to recover.

After a few minutes of existential dread about my career, my sad girl playlist is interrupted by a phone call.

I pick it up to my sister's overly chipper voice.

"What time are you coming tomorrow?" she asks and I groan.

"I don't know, Mel, this week has been exhausting."

"C'mon, just come and stay for the weekend. You can pretend you're super rich and just going away to the cottage for the weekend."

I laugh at that. "As if I'll ever be able to afford a cottage."

"Exactly! So take the opportunity while you can," she says. I sigh and she interrupts me before I can decline again, "Please? I didn't see you last weekend and Liam is asking about you. I need some sibling bonding time after the week I've had."

"Okay," I eventually agree.

"Why don't you bring Bea? Maybe she wants a getaway from the city too," Mel says.

She probably means it to be helpful, but as I haven't told her about what happened last weekend, she doesn't realize what that suggestion does to me.

Bea and I have been acting civil and friendly this week but I'm trying not to spend too much time in her vicinity. I don't want it to be awkward and I'm worried that, every time I look at her, I probably have heart eyes that I can't quite get rid of just yet. Maybe a weekend in the company of others will help me get over it.

"Sure, I'll go ask."

I step out to the living room, where Bea is curled up reading on the couch. During my lunch break, she told me she had to get through this book to provide a review from a bookseller's perspective for some magazine, so I've been trying to give her uninterrupted reading time.

"Melanie is inviting us up to her place this weekend. Want to come? I don't know if you're working or not but she has it in her head that it'll be like a cottage getaway for us."

Bea lowers her book and stares at me over the pages.

"Well, I am free since I get every other weekend off. Will I finally get to meet the nephew I've heard so much about?"

"Of course," I say.

"Okay, I'm in." She smiles and turns back to her book.

"You hear that? I hope you have room for two," I say to Mel as I head back to my room.

I know better than to interrupt the serious business of a good book.

"Duh. You're okay with sharing a bed, right?"

The train ride up north is fast, and while Bea reads, I listen to Chappell Roan and continue the crochet narwhal I'm working on for Liam. I mess up a stitch and have to go back at least twice but I am feeling pretty confident in my attempt to get back into the hobby. I wonder when I became someone who just makes it through the day instead of trying to enjoy it, and I shake away the thought. I try to distract myself by focusing on the album but the song changes from an upbeat tune to one about being mad at someone who claims things are casual but takes you home to meet their family.

I skip to the next song.

The announcement chimes from above, notifying passengers that the next stop is our station and I tap Bea's arm to signal that we need to get off soon.

At the station, Chris is waiting to pick us up. He's standing next to his SUV and waves when he spots us getting off the train. We tap our transit cards at the payment terminal and head his way.

"Wow, my own sister couldn't be bothered to meet me?" I ask as I hug him.

"Nice to see you too, Steph."

"Hi, I'm Bea," Bea says and waves.

He pulls her in for a hug, wrapping her in his large arms.

"So glad to meet you! I've heard so much about you from Steph and my wife."

"Thanks for having me. I hope only good things? I haven't seen Melanie in a while so I'm excited to catch up."

The conversation pauses as Chris loads our bags in the trunk and I let Bea take the front passenger seat.

"When was the last time you saw each other?"

"Maybe Mel's baby shower? Steph brought me, since we

became closer friends around that time. I do remember thinking it was odd that you weren't there..."

"Ugh, don't remind me about that. We planned it months in advance, only for my boss to make me go to some client meeting on that day—across the country. I was so pissed but that meeting and promotion got me this house so I guess it wasn't for nothing."

"Right, right." Bea turns to me, her face reading 'oops did I mess everything up'. It's an expression I usually see when we're out with our friends and she accidentally asks them an inappropriately timed question. The last one was when she asked Athena about their new beau in front of CJ... I had to do more damage control than necessary on that one.

"So, my favourite brother-in-law—"

"Your only brother-in-law—" he interrupts.

"My dear sweet, one and only brother-in-law... what's for dinner?"

"You heathen. You already know it's going to be from Taj's."

"Yessss! My prince, my knight in shining armour." I lean forward and plant a kiss on his cheek. Nothing quite like my favourite restaurant to cheer me up.

"Thank your sister." He rolls his eyes, but they betray his smile.

"Good restaurant?" Bea asks.

"The best," I confirm.

We pull up to the house a few minutes later and I make sure to compliment Chris on the great yard work. This garden is his pride and joy, and Bea picks up the vibe because she does the same.

When Chris turns away to point out his new hydrangeas, I give Bea a thumbs-up, which she returns with a wink.

Just as I debate making a run for it into the house by pretending that I need to pee, the door opens and the most adorable toddler runs out.

"Aunt Steph!"

"Hey, bud," I say as Liam tumbles into me. "You feeling better this weekend?"

"Yes, we're all better." Mel walks down the porch stairs and comes in for a hug.

"Let's go and set the table. I'm hungry," I say and drag them inside.

As I wash my hands in the front bathroom, my phone chimes.

> How could you leave me outside like that?

> > You're not enjoying Chris's description of how he bred his award-winning tulips?

> It's not as thrilling as he said it would be.

> > It's okay it'll be over soon. . . he'll move on to the cherry tree next.

> Not sure how that's any better so please come rescue me by saying you have an urgent task for me.

> > Maybe.

I put down my phone and head to the kitchen to see if I can find a reason to insist that Bea should come inside. Seeing as Liam is already working on setting the table with napkins, I stand next to Melanie as she unpacks the takeout boxes.

"You seem happy," she says to me.

"Happy to be off work," I sigh. "This one client has been driving us bonkers. They can't make up their mind about the job posting. We're already a few weeks behind from when we originally needed to go live."

"Fair enough. Work has been hell for me too. . ." She launches into a story about the hiring freeze at her workplace coinciding with the promotion of her white male boss and I shake my head in sympathy.

We move on to gossip about her other friends and I get a

sneaking suspicion that I've forgotten to something. My instinct is confirmed as Bea and Chris walk in, both sweating a little from the afternoon sun.

"Hey, Melanie!" Bea runs over to her to give her a hug. "Sorry it took me a while. Your husband was keeping me hostage."

She turns to me as she says this last part, and I give her an apologetic smile.

"It's okay, Chris has a habit of doing that with all new visitors. It's been too long since I've seen you. What are you up to these days?" Mel asks as she carries the food over to the dining table.

I trail behind, holding the other dishes.

The conversation at dinner flows smoothly and Liam only interrupts occasionally to chime in with his opinion about what's new in his life. We learn all about his beginner skating classes, his classmates, and his favourite *Bluey* characters.

When he leaves the table to go watch some TV (after receiving his parents' permission, of course), Mel turns back to us conspiratorially.

"Great, now time for the adult conversation. Bea, can you please convince Steph to start dating again? I need some good news to report to our mom so she stays off my case."

"Why is Mom on your case? She hasn't mentioned anything to me."

Considering we text fairly regularly, I assume it would've come up by now. Mostly, our texts revolve around "I'm still alive" or "sorry I missed your call, I was working."

"She doesn't want to bother you about it. She has a theory that the hands-off approach works because that's how I met Chris. I didn't tell her about him until the last possible moment."

"Well, apologies to you and your mom, but there's no convincing this one," Bea says, wrapping an arm around my shoulder from where she sits next to me.

I lean into her, finding comfort in her embrace. This is why I value our friendship; she knows exactly what I need, and right now, I definitely need a buffer for this conversation.

"The work excuse isn't just an excuse," I say.

Melanie sighs dramatically, taking a sip of the single wine glass she allows herself on these weekends.

"Well, what about you, Bea? Maybe you can set a good example for my wayward sister."

It takes considerably more effort than I thought to stay silent at that.

"Not sure I'm a good benchmark to compare to. My dating results have been varied."

"Varied?"

"You know, some good, some bad."

Melanie claps her hands together. "Okay, perfect, tell us all about the good ones so you can inspire Steph to find something similar."

Bea removes her arm from where it was curled around me and grabs a sip from her own wine glass.

"Well, there haven't been that many good ones. Definitely more misses than hits."

"Stop mixing your metaphors and just get on with it. Did you at least have sex with the last one?"

The question causes me to choke on air but I expertly cover it up with a cough. Chris raises an eyebrow at me but Melanie is giving Bea her full attention and she ignores my outburst.

I glance towards Bea for her answer, trying to maintain a very stoic expression. Chris continues to glance at me curiously from where he's sitting across from me so I realize I likely failed.

"Yes, but it wasn't exactly with the original date. The first date ended in disaster."

"Even more impressive! Two dates in one night. Was the second one good?"

Bea shrugs but I can see a smile in her expression. If I wasn't here, would she tell them more? *Stop dreaming, Steph*, I chide myself.

"That's what you need to aim for." Mel turns back to me. "Two dates in one night, so you can have a little competition between them in your mind. You know how much you like rankings and competition. Think of it as a job recruitment."

"Thanks, but no thanks. Do you know much work it is to find one person to date, let alone two?"

"Well, which date did you like more?" Chris turns to ask Bea.

"Obviously the second if they slept together," Melanie says.

I hope my face remains as neutral as I want it to.

"Of course," Chris agrees, glancing at me out of the corner of his eye.

Oh God, they're definitely going to find out, aren't they?

Thankfully, the conversation diverts as Melanie's phone pings, distracting her. When she turns back to the table, we've already moved on to discussing the latest season of our favourite sci-fi show.

When it's clear that we're all too full to keep eating, I help Chris wash the dishes, while Mel and Bea take their wine glasses over to the living room where they can continue to catch up. Chris is on rinsing duty and I dutifully load them into the dishwasher as he hands me the rinsed plates.

"You okay after that conversation?"

"What do you mean?"

"You know how your sister is; she can get a bit pushy."

"That's true, but it's nothing I haven't heard before," I say honestly. "She has been wanting me to date for a while."

"It's only because she worries about you," he says.

"Oh yes, poor me, all alone in the big city," I joke.

"Well, not so alone, right?" He raises an eyebrow, pausing the fast rinsing he's been doing.

"No, not all alone," I confirm.

"Bea seems nice," he adds.

"She is," I respond.

"Second date nice?" He turns off the tap as he hands me the last plate.

"Huh? Whatever do you mean?" I grab the plate and feign ignorance.

Don't look at him, do not make eye contact.

"You know what I mean. You think I haven't figured out how to read the signature Richards embarrassed face?"

"I don't know what you're talking about. Melanie and I are nothing alike." At least this answer is a natural one.

"That's true, but you have the same expressive faces."

"If you say so..."

He grabs me by the shoulder and drags me back towards the dining room table. I lean past him to glance towards the living room, where I can see Bea and Mel still sitting on the couch, now listening as Liam regales them with a story that involves teddy bear acting.

"Melanie is not the only one worried about you. Is that what's been going on? You seemed a bit nervous at dinner," he says as he sits me down at the dining room table so we can have our own conversation.

I figure, if he's found out already, maybe I can at least ask him for advice. Cheri already shared all her wisdom, and while I appreciate her efforts at trying to get me to open up, talking to her that one time on the phone was the best I could do. It seems opening that trap door that's been shut in my mind has spilled out to other areas, and as much as I want to avoid thinking about it, now that work has been put away, it's the only thing I can think about.

"It was just one night but we've already agreed that it won't happen again. We've been friends for so long. I can't lose that... I can't."

"That's fair, but is that what you mutually agreed on?" Chris says calmly, as if trying to herd a scared cat.

I don't blame him, since this is probably the most I've spoken to him about anything that doesn't involve his wife or his plants.

"It wasn't my idea, if that's what you're getting at. I did agree to it, though. It's sound logic."

"You do enjoy your logic, most of the time."

I smile at that.

"But something tells me you don't want to be logical in this case."

"I know what you're trying to say and I appreciate you, but let's keep this between ourselves. I'm handling it so well, as you can see, so let's not make it worse."

"You got it, champ." He claps me on the shoulder in a classic bro move and I snort at the ridiculousness.

"Is that what you whisper to your plants to cheer them up?"

"No, I usually tell them to follow their heart but I don't think this particular plant wants to hear it." He claps me on the shoulder again and walks away.

I watch as he adorably tiptoes towards his son, making childish giggles erupt from the living room as he tickles Liam from the behind.

I stop to grab another glass of water, knowing I'll have to steel myself for the rest of the evening. *You can do it, Steph, you can survive the rest of the night in a calm fashion.*

∽

I can't do it.

I lied to myself. There is no singular way I can survive tonight. *Please smite me right here, please just take me out.*

The one bed was not the issue, that was fine. I mean, it is a full bed but I had to lie down at the very edge of my side just in case (I do not want Bea feeling uncomfortable) so we are at least two inches apart.

Scrolling in silence in the dark on our phones is something we've done many times over the years.

It's just that... the glow of her iPad distracted me away from my phone and I can see that she's reading a particularly spicy scene. I don't think my imagination can take it. The main character is describing a very interesting scenario in which she finds herself trapped in the elevator with a one-night stand, clothes are being discarded and—

"Whatcha reading?" I try to ask neutrally.

Bea lowers the brightness of her iPad screen and turns towards me. "Oh sorry, was the brightness too high? I can turn it off if you're going to sleep."

"No, no, don't worry. What's the book? It seemed. . . interesting."

"Oh, it's just an ARC from a publisher for a new queer rom-com."

"An ark?"

"A-R-C. Advanced Reader's Copy. I get them for the bookstore so I know what to stock."

"Oh right, you've mentioned that before. Is this particular one any good?"

"It's entertaining so far but I'm not quite sure yet. *Someone* interrupted me before I could finish the chapter."

"I don't know how you can read that with a straight face."

"It's easy. See, look." Bea turns towards me completely, placing the iPad slightly beneath her so I can watch her face as she reads.

Despite what I can imagine is going on in those pages, her expression remains pretty neutral. You'd think she was reading a dictionary, and I'm impressed.

"Wow, no one would be able to tell that you're reading pure smut like that."

"Years of working retail have given me quite a good poker face." She laughs. "I've mastered controlling my facial expressions."

"Just the facial expressions? Other parts of you are reacting?"

She continues to read but responds to the question.

"If that's your weird way of asking me if reading makes me occasionally horny then the answer is obviously. But don't worry, this is only a light scene and it'll pass."

"You don't have to. I mean, you should act on your instincts."

Bea turns off the screen and looks up at me with an eyebrow raised.

"Please clarify," she says, the poker face still on.

"I mean, if you feel a type of way... you could take care of it. I wouldn't mind," I say, aiming for her level of neutrality.

"Are you sure?"

"I mean, I could help?" I hope the question doesn't come out as breathless as I imagine it to be.

"That's probably not a good idea," she says but moves her iPad behind her on the bed so there's nothing separating us.

I take a few deep breaths, studying her face.

"Probably, but it could be fun," I settle on.

It takes her a few moments to respond but I watch as a mischievous smile appears.

"What did you have in mind?" she finally asks.

"You can keep reading, and I'll just help."

She searches my face as she thinks about it. Whether it's the look in my eyes or something else, she responds after a silent minute. "Okay, but just for today. I have to admit I'm curious about what you have in mind."

I can agree to those terms, so I nod. "Sit up, please?"

She does as I ask, propping up a pillow against the headboard as she lounges against it. When she's ready, she holds her iPad in her hand and raises an eyebrow at me, daring me to make the next move.

"Spread your legs," I ask as I sit up.

She does and I move so I'm between them.

"Start reading."

As she reads, I lower myself to her left thigh, kissing my way up. When I reach her centre, I am delighted to find it ready for me. Her taste is what I've missed most this past week and I find it just as intoxicating as the first time. My tongue goes slow, wanting to savour the moment and I am rewarded with a moan for my efforts.

"F-faster, please."

I feel her caress my hair. I glance up and see she's no longer reading, her device thrown to the side. I pull away for a moment and she reaches towards me.

"What happened to reading?" I ask.

"This is admittedly more fun," Bea replies, dragging me up for a kiss.

She must taste herself on my lips but she says nothing and I lean into the kiss, almost wanting to ask why we didn't just start there. As she kisses me, I continue my work from earlier, using my hand this time.

She returns the favour and now we're just kissing each other messily, hands reaching and grasping and hips moving to chase our pleasure further. It doesn't take long for my own body to react, the thoughts I've been suppressing this past week finally rising to the surface. I feel her core tighten around my hand and I kiss her through the high. When mine starts, I can't hide the soft sighs that come out and Bea smiles as she kisses me through it; a kiss on my neck, one on my cheek, and an open-mouthed kiss on my lips.

As our breathing evens out, I pull away and stare into her eyes. Does she know how captivating she is in these intimate moments? I still can't trace the moment I began to look at her with this kind of wonder, but now I've started, I don't know how I could ever stop. No wonder everyone can read my hopelessness on my face.

I have no clue what she's thinking as she returns my breathless stare, but whatever it is must be somewhat nice as she gives me a quick peck.

"Thank you," she whispers.

I don't want to say 'you're welcome', as that would be weird. I mean, I did propose this as a favour, but whether for her or for myself, I'm not quite sure yet.

I smile and move back towards my side of the bed, unsure of what to say. It isn't awkward per se but I definitely don't know what to say to my best friend who I just got off, again, even after we agreed a few days ago that it would not happen again. . . But when it comes to her, how can I stay away?

Bea clears her throat and lies down next to me, tucking herself into my side as she's done so many times. Is this still as platonic as it was all those other times? I try to focus on the pleasure of the last few minutes instead of the confusion that will undoubtedly find me tomorrow.

I close my eyes, trying to even out my breathing. Bea snuggles in closer and I shift so I'm lying at my side, wrapping her in a hug. *This is nice*, I decide.

"What are we going to do about these sheets?" she whispers, making me laugh.

"Don't worry, I'll just start the laundry in the morning." I give her a forehead peck, trying to smooth out the concerned wrinkle that has now appeared there.

"Good night, Steph." She smiles and closes her eyes.

My heart warms at the sight and I don't even have the energy to mentally scold myself. *I am definitely in trouble.*

∽

"Hmm, what am I looking at here?" Melanie asks as she walks into the mudroom where I have just finished loading last night's bedsheets into the washer.

"What do you mean? I'm helping you with your housework like a great sister."

"Exactly. That's why it's so suspicious."

I laugh, aiming for a nonchalant arm pat that comes across even more weird.

"I'm just trying to show you my appreciation," I settle on.

"Ooohkay," Mel finally says, shaking her head as she leaves the room.

Phew. I'm glad it was Mel who found me and not Chris. He would buy my reasoning even less than her. I turn on the machine and hear footsteps behind me, expecting it to be Chris (with my luck), but when I turn back to see who it is, it's Bea who stands in the doorway. She smiles.

"You weren't joking about the laundry," she says, holding out a mug towards me. It's Earl Grey, of course.

"Thanks," I say when I finish a lengthy gulp. "This is exactly what I needed."

"Me too," she says, but before I have time to ask what she's referring to, Liam runs in.

"Aunt Steph, let's go play Mario Kart!"

"What else would we do today?" I ask as I let him grab my free hand and drag me away.

Later, the ride back to the city is comfortable, despite my clear efforts to avoid thinking about or discussing last night's events in more detail. Bea must be doing the same because it is decidedly the one thing we do not talk about, though my mind drifts to it every now and again and I have to stop myself from letting my thoughts linger there for fear that she'll be able to see it on my face.

For dinner, I order pizza because there's no way I want to cook today and I order enough for us both to be able to have leftovers for tomorrow. No one warns you how much of your day as an adult gets spent cooking and cleaning, and the late spring weather makes me want to avoid any semblance of chores. Dinner is pleasant enough, but I have to avoid thinking too long about the satisfied sounds Bea makes as she eats. Being around her every meal for the past week has made me notice it and I can usually ignore it, but combined with last night, it's fodder for the filthy part of my brain and I have to tune it out.

As Bea tidies up the dishes (as a thank you for the pizza), I wash my face and get ready for bed. I make a mental note to remember to come back to brush my teeth and I leave Bea to it in the living room, closing my bedroom door behind me. It's not that I necessarily want to distance myself but I know how it is to sleep in the living room; any moment of privacy is important.

And after the weekend, I should probably take a minute to myself.

Headphones in, crochet needle in hand... this is the life. As I take a picture of the narwhal to update Melanie on the project, I hear a knock at the door. I take out a single earbud.

"Yes?" I ask.

Bea opens the door, holding her blanket and now in her pyjamas.

"Can I sleep in here?"

"Of course," I respond quickly, trying to calm my ever-fast beating heart whenever she's around. *It's just sleep, you delinquent.*

"Thank you. After last night's soft bed, I think I need a break from the couch."

"I told you from the start that it was silly for you to sleep there."

She rolls her eyes as she settles in next to me on her side of the bed.

"Yes, yes, you told me so... blah blah. I'm going to read a bit on my phone before I fall asleep, but don't bother waking me up if I fall asleep almost immediately."

Her soft request is punctuated by a yawn so I smile and put my headphones back in to keep working on my project.

She's right; it doesn't take long for her to pass out with her phone in her hand. As quietly as I can, I slip out of the bed to turn out the lights and put away my things. I also grab her phone and put it on the nightstand before tiptoeing out to go brush my teeth. When I slip back into bed a few minutes later, she turns towards me and it takes more effort than I thought possible to resist curling up next to her and scooping her into my arms. If I thought it was difficult to be around her before, I am in a whole new realm of torture now.

CHAPTER FIVE

The next few days pass by amicably and Bea continues to sleep in my bed. It's nice, *too* nice. On the third night, she asks to cuddle while we watch a movie on my laptop, and because I'm a pushover when it comes to her, I agree and tell myself I will keep it platonic.

The next night, the cuddle happens again with a chaste goodnight kiss on my cheek and I nearly faint.

By Friday, I find myself eagerly looking forward to the evening and our inevitable time together. I spend my lunch break thinking about it, my mind wandering as I take a break from the mandatory training Jeff called us in for on our usual work-from-home day.

I know we said we weren't dating but it feels more and more like dating every night. Our morning texts are filled with hearts and "have a great day at work!" but that's normal for us. That's how we've always spoken to each other in our friendship. But do the hearts have more significance now? I can't be the only one who's confused. But I don't think I can handle another rejection. And I don't want to lose her. *Ugh.*

"You doing okay there, dear?" Cheri asks.

I guess that internal groan was not as internal as I thought.

"Yes, all good over here," I reply as I continue to dig into my salad.

I should spend less of my lunch break stewing and more of it actually chewing. I almost laugh at the little rhyme in my head.

"Is it that Hope Valley case? I know the client's been a bit picky."

"Oh, that's fine. I mean, it's a little annoying but a few phone calls a day isn't the end of the world."

"But something else is?" She raises an eyebrow at me over her phone.

She tends to spend her breaks catching up on her notifications. Cody usually has an update or two about his school day for her.

"Just things at home."

"Oh yes, *that*."

"I'm not quite sure I like your emphasis there."

"No, what you really don't like is being around someone you want but can't really have. You can't have your cake and eat it too, at least not based on the boundaries you told me the two of you agreed on."

"I know, I know. You don't need to remind me. But she makes it really hard. I can't help but imagine something more." I sigh.

"That's all it is though right now, imagination. There's no action," she tells me bluntly.

"Damn, did you really need to read me like that?" Though I know she's right, it hurts to hear it spelled out that way. "I mean... there's been some action," I correct.

She raises an eyebrow at me again and puts her phone down, putting her hands together in a serious way.

"I don't think I want to know," she starts. "I think y'all need to communicate with words. I know you're probably scared because you don't want to ruin whatever you have going on, since it's easier to ignore issues than confront them. But you need to talk and have an actual conversation. You can't stay in the same spot and expect progress to take place."

I sigh and put my head in my hands.

"Stop being so smart and wise, it's making my head hurt."

"Your head probably already hurts from the whiplash your heart is doing."

I mimic a stabbing wound to my chest.

"Wow, just cut me even further, why don't you?"

Cheri laughs.

"Trust me, if I really wanted to cut you, I'd talk about those shoes because, baby, what closet did you drag those crusty loafers from?"

I laugh with her, grateful for the subject change.

The subway ride is quite smooth for once, without any delays, and I return home shortly before 6pm. I know Bea's usually home on Friday afternoons, but for some reason, I'm still surprised to see her resting on the couch.

"You're home early," I say as I walk in, leaving my work backpack at the entryway to my bedroom.

"I'm always home at this time on Fridays," she says, smiling at my apparent forgetfulness.

"Oh, that's right. Sorry, my day's been hectic."

"I totally get it. Let's go out to kick off the weekend? There's a new Thai restaurant I've been dying to try and I think the hype has died down so there should hopefully be no line."

The idea sounds like a perfect distraction from my jumbled thoughts, and I agree to it. As we've been taking turns cooking and clearing the dishes in smooth domestic bliss, it seems special to go out. A nice little treat at the end of the week.

As it's only a thirty-minute walk away from my place, we decide to walk over. Toronto in the spring is my favourite time. While there's more tourists than usual, the nice weather and walkability make it so fun to stroll everywhere.

A light breeze filters through the air as we walk and our

smooth conversation resembles the lightness in the air. As we walk closer to each other to avoid the tourists passing by, I debate grabbing Bea's hand. I'm trying not to read too much into the outing but the smile on Bea's face is definitely giving date vibes, though I'm wishing for it to be one so badly that perhaps I'm imagining it.

While the restaurant is quite full, there are small tables for two and we're seated immediately upon arrival towards the back of the restaurant. With its dim lighting and fake candle at the centre of the table, the scene is quite intimate and I don't apologize when my leg accidentally brushes against Bea's and rests there.

"To making it to the end of the week." Bea raises her glass of pop in a toast.

"Hear, hear," I agree and clink my own with hers.

After we place our order with the friendly server who led us in, I'm back to staring at Bea. It should be awkward; she should be looking away or at her phone but she just smiles at me and I can tell her brain is working on a conversation topic.

"So, how was work?" is what she settles on.

"Good. We're almost done wrapping up that big recruitment so I'm excited to be done with those daily calls. What about you? What new display idea are you thinking of doing?"

"I'm not sure yet. I think I may let Brodie decide on the display."

"Wow, that's big of you. I know you hate to give up control like that."

In all the years I've known Bea, she has never let anyone else touch her precious book babies. Exceptions have been granted for birthdays, an occasional promotion, or if someone has buttered her up enough for months on end. The last one she gave was assigned after many months of her favourite iced coffee and a slice of banana bread brought to her any time she sat in the back office.

"They've been doing really well lately. The F&B manager told me that the customers have been complimenting them like there's no tomorrow. I know it's been an adjustment for them so I think this will cheer them up. They've been talking about doing a display for fiction featuring non-binary authors and characters."

"That's a great idea." I smile at her thoughtfulness.

Moments like this remind me why I like her so much and I have to take a sip of my drink to wash down the thought. *We are not going there, Steph*, I remind myself.

Bea's leg rubs against me and the light in her eyes makes me want to throw it all away. *Should I just say something?*

"Bea, there's something I need to talk to you about," I say, mustering up every ounce of courage I can. I've totally got this.

"That sounds totally cool and not at all threatening or mysterious," she teases, laughing softly at her own joke.

"It's not that deep," I assure her, perhaps lying. I take a deep breath. *You can do it, being vulnerable is totally simple and easy. You can—*

My inner monologue is interrupted by a buzzing from Bea's purse.

"One second," she says, reaching into her bag and pulling out her phone.

"Oh, it's Seema, my roommate. I should take this." She looks apologetic as she answers the phone.

I awkwardly smile in an 'it's-fine-I-wasn't-about-to-say-anything-important' way and she whispers into the phone. Thankfully, it's not too loud in here so she doesn't have to step outside, but it's still awkward for one person to be on the phone while the other sits there.

Or maybe it's just me.

"Uh-huh."

"Okay, I'll be there tomorrow."

"Thanks for letting me know, talk soon."

She finally hangs up after a few nods and I smile that awkward smile again, "Everything okay?" I ask.

"Yes, actually, it's great news. The toilet was fixed much earlier than I thought it would be. Apparently, they just brought the new one over earlier today. Seema got an email from the landlord.

She's on her way to check it out now and she'll text me whether it's actually all fixed. If it is, I can go back to my place."

My heart drops.

"Oh, that's great news." I hope my tone is much happier than I feel.

I'm trying to be rational. While it was great having her with me, she does need her own place. *I am happy for her*, I try to convince myself.

She smiles wide. "I can't wait to go home to my books! No offence to my Kindle, but I keep seeing TikToks about this one book I have in physical copy at home."

"I'm sure your books will be happy to see you too." I laugh.

The rest of the dinner flows smoothly and I ignore the sinking feeling in my chest. It's unfair of me to wish for something other than her happiness, and if returning to her place is what will make her happy, then so be it.

When we get back to my place, I help Bea pack her tiny suitcase and we laugh over how much her stuff has taken over my bathroom.

"I'll keep my toothbrush out for the morning," she says as she places it back in the holder our toothbrushes have been sharing. It's so domestic, I don't know what to do with myself.

"You're going to stay tonight?"

"Yeah, even if Seema says everything is fine, I want to go in the morning because that food took me out. I'm way too tired to think about commuting back across the city right now."

"Fair enough." As always, her logic is flawless.

"Can I borrow some pyjamas, though? I just packed mine." She laughs in her usual self-deprecating way and I mentally catalogue the sound as something I will miss. Where's Cheri to slap some sense into me when I need it?

Not wanting Bea to wear anything too dishevelled, I lend her a pair of sweatpants and a keshi T-shirt. I've seen her in my borrowed clothes before, many times. Especially in our university days when we would be too lazy to go back to our rooms after a long study and reading session. But something about seeing her in them now. . . I need a cold shower to remind myself there's no special meaning behind it.

"It's a little baggy but not too bad. Thank you!" she says as she lies back on the couch, scrolling on her phone.

If I was braver than I am, I'd say something. Invite her back to my bed. Confront the blissful past few days in which I've been able to pretend her gestures were anything more than friendly comfort. Stake my claim like those dominant romance heroes Bea is always talking about. But I'm not any of those things; I'm just hopelessly besotted and anxious. The opposite combination of a successful romance lead. I must sigh a little too loudly because she looks up at me from her comfy position on the couch.

"You okay?"

"Yes, of course, just remembered something about work," I lie.

"Ew, work is for Monday. Let's just relax today." She sits up. "Should we watch a movie?"

"As long as it's not horror." I join her on the couch when she shifts to make room for me.

It takes us far too long to choose what to watch as we both insist on seeing a movie that neither of us have seen before and it turns out that everything I suggest she's already seen and vice versa. By the time we finally hit play, I'm already yawning and it doesn't take long for me to end up curled up against Bea.

"This is nice," she says as I struggle to stay awake.

"Yes, it is." I draw out the last word with a yawn.

CHAPTER SIX

Once Bea leaves, it takes no time at all for us to go back to our pre-spring routine; texting once a day to check in and sending photos when we see something that reminds us of the other person. It's only been a few days but it feels longer, our closeness severed so suddenly.

I know I'm being ridiculous. I know that. But now that I've had a taste of what things could be, I can't convince myself to pretend that it didn't happen.

Cheri must sense it too because she invites me out to a happy hour on Thursday after our shift.

"There's nothing that cheap food and drinks can't cure," is what she said when she invited me, and I tend to agree.

So here we are, yelling over the too-loud music after our server takes our order.

"So, let it out, what has you all mopey this week? I'm pretty sure I can guess but I want to hear it from you," she says.

"If you can guess, why don't you just tell me what I can do to fix it, so I can go back to my normal self?" I sigh.

"Well, do you think the way you've been acting over the past few months is normal? You were working all the time and stress-dreaming about emails. That's why Jeff and I got you that company dinner, to make you think about something other than work for once."

"I appreciate that but I'm not sure this is much better. Now all I think about is what I can't have. Maybe ignorance is really bliss." I put my head in my hands and sigh again.

"This is so pitiful. Seriously, as your work mom, I can't stand to watch this." She shakes her head. She's about to say something else when we're interrupted by the server bringing our drinks.

I stave off the incoming pity party by taking a sip of my mocktail, having decided I don't want to deal with a headache tomorrow, since it is technically a workday.

"I'm not sure I appreciate being called pitiful. I've been called many things, but pitiful is not one I'd like to add to my list."

"Well, it's the truth. You could fix your doom-and-gloom attitude by just being honest with Bea and telling her you love her."

"Love seems pretty strong to start with." I blank at the thought of actually saying those words.

"I don't know what else you'd call it," Cheri says. "But what's the worst that can happen if you tell her and she doesn't reciprocate?"

"I wouldn't be telling her I love her, but if I did say something about how maybe we should probably date and if she doesn't feel the same. . . We'd probably stop being friends and then she wouldn't be in my life at all."

"Or she could feel the same and then you'd be riding off on a unicorn into the sunset together," Cheri responds.

"Is that what happened when you and your wife got together?"

"Well, we rode something else but the sentiment is similar." She laughs.

I laugh at the crude joke.

"You're horrible," I say when the giggles die down.

"Not as horrible as you're being to yourself by denying how you truly feel." She sips her drink with a *gotcha* look.

Ouch.

"Wow. Just wow," is all I can say.

"There, there, buttercup. You're too young to be dealing with all this emotional whiplash. Just be honest. Either say it or move on. This middle ground will only hurt you."

She's right; I know she's right and I guess I just needed an emotional kicking to really grasp it. I am too young to be this miserable. I think. When did I start thinking that I didn't deserve the happiness I want to see for other people?

Before I can begin to unpack the train of thought or overthink it, I down my drink and slam the glass onto the table. Easy to do when the sting of alcohol that usually accompanies such a gesture is missing.

"Okay, I'll go tell her."

"Atta girl!" Cheri cheers. "Get it while the night is young."

"I still don't know if anything will be gotten, but I'll at least try and be honest."

"Honesty is the first step, and hopefully by tomorrow, you'll at least have the answer you need. If all else fails, I'll sign you up on a dating app tomorrow."

"Thank you, but no thank you," I say earnestly as I dig through my backpack for my credit card. "If it's taken me this long to tell my long-term crush how I feel about her, I don't think I'll be ready for the apps overnight."

"Well, as our queen Dua Lipa says, the best way to get over someone is to get underneath someone else."

I shake my head at her logic as our server appears after I flag them down. Once I pay for us both (the least Cheri can get after her sage advice is a free drink), I give her a peck on the cheek.

"Thank you. You're the best work mom ever."

"No problem, go get her. And thanks to you, now I can invite Phoebe to join me for her own post-work treat." She winks.

I can't say anything to that other than shake my head, so I do and head out.

I'm panting as I run up to Love A Latte Books, and not in a sexy way. The TTC was moving slower than usual due to some unexplainable track work and the trains were so busy that I had to wait for three to pass by before I dared get on.

I look through the glass windows, where I can see Bea talking to Brodie at the barista station. Good, she's distracted. I step away a bit to catch my breath and smooth down my hair. I check my phone for the time; 10 minutes until closing.

I walk in and pretend to browse the table at the front that features queer pop icons. I'm flipping through a picture book about Elton John when I hear a throat clearing next to me. I turn, expecting it to be Bea, but it's Brodie.

"We're closing in five," they say in a voice I can tell is reserved for customers.

"Oh, hey, Brodie. Is Bea around?"

"She's closing up tonight, so I can go tell her you're waiting?" they offer.

"Sure, thank you."

I awkwardly move to the side and watch as customers pack up their stuff and leave. I pretend to be scrolling through something on my phone until it's just myself and Brodie at the front of the store. The situation is starting to mirror the last time I followed Bea to work, when she told me she wanted us to remain just friends. Oh God, am I setting myself up for similar disappointment?

"Beatrice wanted me to tell you she's taking care of something at the back, so you can go meet her in the manager's office. Just lock the front doors when I leave, okay?" Brodie says as they approach.

They're carrying a tote bag with their band name embroidered in silver thread, clearly on their way out.

"No problem," I say and follow them to the door.

They step out and wait on the other side. I lock the doors and they leave with a wave, after testing that the door is indeed locked.

Now it's just me and the twenty-second walk to the manager's office, which I assume is at the back of the store behind the door that's marked 'Staff Only'. *You've got this, Steph.*

I take a deep breath and open the door, which leads to another hallway. There are several rooms on the left side of the hallway, and to the right, there's a few coat hooks and book carts full of new stock. I pass the first door, a washroom. The second door reveals a small office with filing cabinets and a desk with a desktop computer on it. The office chair is empty.

"Bea?" I call out to the empty hallway.

"Over here!" I hear her reply from the last room in the hallway.

I enter the room to see that it has a small kitchen set up to the right, and the left has boxes and boxes of what I assume is book stock.

"This room is like the TARDIS. I swear this hallway looks bigger on the inside," I call out, not seeing Bea yet.

"It is, isn't it? Though I'm not sure how safe it is to have the extra kitchen right next to the books," Bea agrees as she steps out from the room's depths.

It's only been a few days since I've seen her but seeing her now in person reminds me how besotted I am with her. How does she manage to look this good after a long day at work? My stomach flutters at the thought of what I want to say.

"Sorry to keep you waiting. I was responding to an email about a local author's book signing next week and then I had to count the stock to make sure we had enough copies so, anyway, now I'm here."

She gestures around the room.

"No worries. I've never been in here before. It's cool. I guess there's probably a lot about bookstore management that I know nothing about."

"That's okay... Well, what's up?" she asks.

I sense the actual question behind her words; why am I here, all of a sudden? Oy, how do I begin to answer that?

"Well, I was out with Cheri, and while it was really nice, I realized I wanted to be here with you. Well, not here, but you know, where you were. Which happens to be here. And so, now I'm here."

I aim for a ta-da gesture but I'm sure it comes out as awkward as it was to say. I haven't felt this dorky in a while and I feel a blush forming on my cheeks.

"You're so cute," Bea says, coming to stand in front of me.

"C-cute?" I'm trying to process her being close again. Her usual lavender perfume, while definitely faded, lingers in the air in front of me.

"That was a really sweet way to say you miss me. You can just say that, you know." She smiles.

"I miss you," I say at her prompt. Her smile is infectious, and I allow myself to smile back.

"I've missed you too. I mean, don't get me wrong, I like being around all my own things and the furniture I curated and, oh gosh—my bed. But I miss being around you too," she responds.

"Well, since we clearly miss each other, maybe we can hang out more often," I suggest.

"Of course! We need to start planning our summer activities."

"I meant, like, in a non-platonic way. Like, we should date because you standing so close to me has me thinking some very non-platonic things."

Bea laughs and grabs my hands, pulling me closer. I really hope she can't feel the extra nervous sweat that has developed there. *Nope, Steph, focus, we are not thinking about sweaty hands right now.*

"Were we not dating before? I mean, what else do you call all that cuddling?" She giggles a little as she studies my confused expression.

"You should tell me, because you're technically the one with more experience in this department."

"Oh, so all the 'taking care of you' talk was inexperience? If that was you at inexperienced, I'd love to see what else I can teach you," she says as she moves closer.

She's so close I can feel her chest brush against mine and I could likely start counting the freckles across her cheeks, if I can focus long enough to look away from her lips.

"Please just kiss me already," she whispers and so, I do.

Where I may have been timid in initiating it, she meets my pace and deepens the kiss. Her hands untangle from mine as she uses her arms to bring me closer into an embrace. I do the same and place my hand under her shirt at the back, cradling her towards me. My right hand reaches towards her bra strap and I pull away just as I'm about to unhook it.

"Wait," I say as I step back, breathing hard. "Should we be doing this here?"

"I wouldn't say we *should,* but we can. I mean, the cameras in this room only monitor the kitchen for food safety reasons. The storage area is quite extensive..."

"Wouldn't the owners know when they see the footage of us kissing and then realize what's probably going on if we go back there?"

"What would be going on?" she asks in what I can tell is her 'innocent' voice. Used in past situations to beg for the last slice of pizza and extra candy at the movies. And now, apparently, make-out sessions.

"Don't use that voice on me."

"What voice?" she asks, stepping closer to me.

"You know..." I can't focus as she hooks her arms around my neck.

She leans up to whisper in my ear, "C'mon, let me show you how much I want you non-platonically too."

I nearly melt at the words and I kiss her softly in response.

"I want nothing more than that but I'd be too worried about getting you in trouble. This job is too important to you and I'd hate to sabotage it in any way, even if we never got caught," I say, despite my lower half fighting for attention.

Bea kisses me gently at that. "That's what I love about you."

I freeze, trying to process the words. Surely, she didn't just mean...

She puts her hands on my cheeks, slowly turning my head from side to side.

"Is your brain short-circuiting right now?"

"I think it may be my heart too," I finally say.

"Well then, let's get you home so I can keep my promise from earlier. I meant what I said," she says.

I blink as she steps away and hurries off, leaving me to follow her out of the room.

After I clear my throat, I call out, "About the love part or the show?"

"Both," she calls back from the front of the hallway. I freeze again and she turns to look over her shoulder at me. "Definitely both."

She smiles wide and I find myself returning it.

We hold hands as we walk into my building and I'm trying not to burst out of my skin. How is she so calm as she presses the elevator button? She steps away as I dig through my backpack for my keys and she follows me inside. We kick our shoes off and I have no time to even think about how to approach the situation when she's kissing me again.

It's a warm, tender kiss and I sink into it. I let her lead me to the couch, where she sits down and tugs me into her lap.

"I could get used to this," I giggle as I get settled.

She returns my smile and I get lost for a few seconds staring at her chocolate brown eyes.

"Please do," she says and leans in for another kiss.

It doesn't take long for her kiss to get more needy, and before I know it, she's tugging at my shirt hem. I hesitate for a moment before following her implicit instructions to remove it. Exposed to her in the daylight (thanks to the beginning of the long Toronto summer), a blush creeps into my cheeks as she stares.

"You're so beautiful." She kisses my collarbone and a soft groan escapes me.

"You are too. You have no idea how long I've dreamed of this," I admit as she looks back at me.

"Oh, really? It wasn't just that night a few weeks ago?" Her tone has her usual curiosity in it, as if she's just uncovered a plot twist in the book she's been reading.

"That was probably when I finally admitted it to myself, but I've always had a bit of a crush on you. Ever since we took that English class together and you corrected my paper with more enthusiasm than I'd ever seen someone have about the word 'complement'."

She laughs. "I can't believe you remember that. I did really care about the proper definitions of words back then, until I realized that's not exactly only what my degree was about."

I can't help but pry back a little too, especially if we're laying everything out about it.

"What about you? When did you start thinking about me that way?"

"I'm not quite sure. Maybe I always compared other people to you subconsciously. I've had some pretty nice dates over the years, but no one ever really made me want to keep seeing them. Asking them how their day went, wondering what they were doing. But I did always think about you that way. . . and you are a pretty good kisser."

"Oh, so it's just physical for you?" I tease, goosebumps working along my arms as we continue to stare at each other, chests no longer pressed against each other.

"Well, that certainly helps. I care about you, your interests, your fears and dreams, and I want to be the one that makes you orgasm. Isn't that what love is?"

"When you say it like that, it sounds so simple," I say.

"Why can't it be simple? Who says love has to be hard?" She

tilts her head in confusion, a look I recognize from whenever I try to explain investments or math to her.

As much as I'm enjoying this conversation, I'm also thinking about something else that's been promised.

"That's true. . . Anyway, can we continue this conversation later so you can start doing that thing with your tongue that you're very good at?"

Bea laughs and reinitiates our kiss, and it doesn't take long for us to end up in my bedroom again, where she insists I relax while she does all the work. My perfectionist nature doesn't allow me to fully give in to this request, so after I reciprocate, we end up cuddling again, enjoying some post-sex bliss. I don't think I'll ever get over the feeling of how perfect she feels in my arms and I snuggle closer to her.

"Well, I guess we'll have to make some announcements to our friends," she says to the ceiling.

"What do you mean?"

"I mean, we'll have to tell them we're girlfriends now and that they should get used to us being insufferably cute around them."

"Insufferably cute, how?"

"You know, hand-holding. Going over to each other's houses instead of our own after hang-out sessions. Changing our contact names in our phones to have little hearts in them. The whole shebang."

I laugh. "Your name in my phone has always had a heart next to it. I add emojis for all my friends. Cheri has a little smiley face wearing glasses next to hers. The heart felt right for you."

"Oh my god, you really are obsessed with me, aren't you?" She gives me a peck on the cheek.

"You're just figuring this out?" I tease back and run my fingers along her leg, pulling her closer so her right leg ends up curled around me.

She smiles and moves closer to me, kissing me on the neck right below my ear. Just as I think about upping the ante, she leans back, staring at me with a smile in her eyes.

"You never did say it back," she says.

"Say what back?" I ask, puzzled.

"That you love me."

"Well, to be fair, you only said that you love something about me. Not me, directly." I think back to the moment and she kisses the frown off my face.

"You know what I mean." She leans back to look at me and I smile at her warmth.

"I love you," I say, meaning every word.

"I love you too," she responds.

Of all the looks I've seen on her face over the years, this one has to be my new favourite. It's the look of love and I want to bottle this feeling forever. She must see something reflected back in my eyes because she smiles wide before giggling and collapsing on my chest.

"Who knew that a toilet breaking would get us together?"

"When you say it like that, it sounds a bit ridiculous." I join in her laughter. "If it ever happens again, you're welcome to stay with me. I'll always have room for you."

"Good, because I'm not planning on going anywhere else. Just you, me, and as many books as I can carry."

"Sounds like a plan. I can clear some of my old books from the shelves in the living room and you can bring yours here."

Bea sits up abruptly, turning back towards me in shock. The sight of her bare breasts distracts me and it takes me a bit to see that she's waiting for a response.

"Huh?" I ask, now looking at her face.

"You're giving me a bookshelf?"

"Oh, of course. Mine only has old schoolbooks and knickknacks on it anyway. It may as well be used to its full potential."

Bea smiles, leans back down to give me another kiss and I can feel her gratitude in it.

"You're welcome, but really, I'm the one who should be thanking you," I say as I break away to catch my breath.

"What do you mean?"

"You've made this place feel like a home for the first time in a while, and I know that feeling will only intensify over time."

"Well, you'd better get used to it because I have no plans of leaving. You're stuck with me now."

Instead of responding, I pour my happiness into a kiss and it doesn't take long for us to exchange more breathless promises, eager to keep building upon the relationship we already have.

EPILOGUE

With a book lover for a girlfriend, it stands to reason that I need to get more into her hobby. This is what has prompted me to join a few different sapphic reading communities on Facebook, and I find myself using the long-neglected social media platform for the first time in a while because of it.

I'm currently reading through the comments on a post I made anonymously, asking for underrated reads, when I hear keys jingling in the front door and Bea walks in. While she still has her own place for now, there's something so satisfying about her using the extra set of keys I let her keep permanently to join me whenever she feels like; which is pretty much most times, these days.

"Hey, babe," she calls out as she puts her jacket on a coat hanger, then walks over to the couch.

I close my phone and stand up to meet her halfway, trapping her in a kiss.

"What brings you here? I thought you were already home," I say as I step away to look at her.

If I'd known she was coming over, I would've changed into something a bit cuter. These threadbare pyjamas are not made for company, hot girlfriends included.

"I was, but I got something in the mail that I had to share with you." She runs back to the front of the apartment where she left her purse, digging through it before bringing the letter to where I'm waiting.

She opens the envelope and holds out the postcard-sized page towards me. "Jenna and Gabriella invited me to their wedding! It says Bea Cohen plus one."

I take a look at the card; the colours are beautiful and I can tell how much care went into the invitation. In the months since our run-in at Love A Latte Books, they've gotten quite close to Bea. I hang out with them occasionally too, and while I'm happy to grow our friendship there, I would say that Bea is more their friend than me. "Well, assuming you don't have another date lined up, I'd be happy to accompany you," I tease.

"That was only that one night. I don't overbook myself these days," Bea teases me right back.

I know she's not serious about having anyone else to date; we became exclusive right away and she deleted the dating app she was using while we were still figuring things out.

I roll my eyes and she kisses me softly on the cheek while I shake my head.

"I'll RVSP for us then, make sure to save the date. I'm actually so excited, not only because of the wedding, but because Jenna told me that they've hired Brodie to sing at the reception."

"No way! Quixotic is making a comeback?"

"No, just Brodie as a wedding singer. They're doing it as a favour to Jenna."

"That's so nice of them. I hope they perform some of their own music."

I got into Quixotic right as they were on hiatus, only listening to them after meeting Brodie. That seems to be my luck with good music, getting into the artists months after they just finished a tour.

"Anyway, what were you doing?" Bea asks as she returns from

putting the invite back in her purse for safekeeping. She glances towards the TV and raises an eyebrow.

"Nothing, just scrolling through my phone..."

"Fair enough. Want to just keep doing that while we couch-rot?"

There is nothing that sounds more perfect, and if I didn't already love her, her knowing me so well would do it all over again. Talking about Quixotic makes us want to listen to them, so Bea plays their last album via the TV while we sit and scroll through our phones.

"Look at how cute this post is," Bea squeals and shoves her phone in my face as I'm taking a phone game break from my book research.

Of course, the post staring back at me is mine, and it's funny seeing my words hidden behind the anonymous member tag.

My girlfriend is really into reading so I want to find some books for us to read together. She's a bookseller so she's read most of the ones I see recommended here often (I have a link to her GR page so I can check lol). Also wouldn't mind getting recommendations for some explicit stuff. I could always use an extra lesson.

"That sounds sweet," I say, trying my best to remain neutral.

"You should take notes," Bea teases, poking my side. "We can read some stuff together. I can get you a great discount at the store."

"Sure, just let me know which books to read and what I owe you and consider it done." I poke her back.

"You're the best, y'know that?" Her face takes on that dreamy look I've come to associate with her thinking about me, and it melts me.

"I know. I even wrote that anonymous post." I laugh, the desire to keep it a secret completely gone if it will keep that look on her face for longer.

She looks at her phone, back to me, and then back to her phone.

"Oh my god. I have to comment again. I mean, I already

commented the first time with some book recommendations, but as a moderator, I know some of the other admins were dying to know if my girlfriend is a reader too, after I mentioned it casually in some other posts recently."

"Sure, do what you must."

I shift to give her more room to snuggle next to me, and I make space for her to lie down against my side. My app refreshes and the new notification pings,

Bea Cohen (admin): My girlfriend told me she wrote this post so please send us your well wishes when you make these recommendations. We need something spicy to re-enact. 😉

I snort-laugh as I read the comment, already seeing that it's getting way more heart reactions than I expected.

"Wow, you are a bit of a celebrity here."

"I know, and they're all going to be so jealous of me," she says.

I smile and focus on watching her interact with the post, rather than scrolling through it myself. I can scroll through the well wishes anytime but seeing her face light up in real time is a memory worth seeing myself.

As if reading my mind, she turns off her phone and places it on the floor next to the couch. She holds out her hand and I pass her my phone so she can place it next to hers. She sits up and turns around, now straddling me.

"Should we get a head start on some of the spicy scene re-enactment? I can tell you what to do. . ." she whispers, running her hands through my hair.

I smile and nod.

"Hmm, what's that look for?" she asks, tracing the smile that I can't seem to shake off.

"Just wondering how I got so lucky. You're the best, y'know that?"

"Yes, I do know." She laughs, returning my smile before she turns serious again. "Now, please be quiet and kiss me so we can start our re-enactment."

Still smiling, I kiss her gently as I try to match the mood she's aiming for. I don't know what's next for us, but whatever it is, I know I wouldn't want to be anywhere but by her side.

THE END

SONG FOR YOU

One wedding meet-cute. Two inspired artists. Sparks are about to fly...

Brodie Bailey is best known as the lead singer and occasional writer for the popular indie band Quixotic but right now, Brodie doesn't want to be known at all. While they've been living in Toronto for the past two years and trying to figure out some stuff, they've been struggling to feel the creative spark they rely on for their work.

But when they meet a painter at their close friends' wedding, they start to realize that maybe that spark isn't gone forever.

Taylor Evans is a painter specializing in wedding portraits and while she loves that part of her work, she's ready to try something new. Enter the gorgeous musician she meets at a client's wedding who generously agrees to let her paint them.

As Brodie and Taylor get closer, they start to realize that their feelings might just be growing into something more than just professional courtesy for a fellow artist.

CHAPTER ONE

It's a beautiful day for a wedding. At least I think so. The sky is a brilliant blue, with only a few clouds in the sky, and there's a slight breeze in the air—the summer humidity hasn't yet set in.

I may have shed a tear or two during the ceremony earlier (okay, several) but I managed to pull it together for my performance. The brides wanted an eclectic selection of music, which included singing a few Broadway hits like "Defying Gravity" but I was able to close out the show with Quixotic's "Forever." It was weird performing it without the rest of the group, and I'm pretty sure I messed up RJ's bridge, but the small crowd seemed to love it anyway.

I'm going over the performance in my head, trying to make sure I remember to write down what I think I missed, when I feel a tap on my shoulder. Technically, I'm supposed to be eating now, but with the rest of my table empty as the wedding guests dance to a perfectly curated playlist, I figured I'd obsess instead.

Turning around in my chair, I'm greeted by none other than the beautiful brides.

"Thank you so much, Brodie, for everything," Jenna says as she pulls me in for a hug.

Seated, our height difference isn't too marked, but if I were to stand, I'd have to crouch down to hug her and my knees already hurt from the feeble attempt I made at dancing on stage earlier.

"Of course! I'm so honoured to be here. Truly," I say, ensuring I make eye contact with Gabriella as well. "You both look amazing. I love how each dress suits your individual personalities."

While Jenna wears a gown worthy of a princess, Gabriella is wearing a sleek, skintight, white dress that accentuates all her curves.

"Thank you, Brodie." Gabriella leans in for a hug this time and I remember to hug her back and not let my surprise show.

It seems that weddings really bring out the mush in everyone, and I've been getting hugs from people left and right.

"Make sure you grab something to eat. You've earned it after that performance," Jenna says.

"That goes for you too," I respond, winking.

Jenna actually opened my brief show with a duet we performed together, dedicated to her new wife. It was absolutely adorable and I hope the internet will do their thing to make it go viral. Not that Jenna's had any shortage of bookings or opportunities in the past few years—it's just that good. If I wasn't performing myself, I'd definitely have recorded it to plaster over all the Broadway forums.

"Wasn't she just amazing?" Gabriella pulls her wife closer and kisses her on the cheek.

"Enough of that. Save it for the honeymoon." I roll my eyes for emphasis, hoping my dig isn't diluted too much by the warm smile I feel coming on.

Jenna shakes my shoulders. "Stop being silly, and go get food."

"Okay, okay." I surrender and stand up to show them that I am indeed getting food.

Gabriella is about to say something when someone calls her from the dance floor and she runs over to them.

"Go join your wife." I motion towards the running bride. "I'll be fine."

Jenna nods and follows her spouse. *So adorable*. I shake my head as I walk away from the lovefest.

On my way to the buffet table, I spot a canvas on an easel and a short cart of painting materials next to it.

The artwork is simply stunning. It's not yet complete but I can tell what it's going to be; a portrait of Jenna and Gabriella against the flower arch they exchanged vows in front of. I can tell the artist has done their research as the brides' faces look perfectly painted, and while the dresses and background are missing a few details at the moment, I can tell it will get there.

A throat-clearing sound behind me forces me to turn away. The offender is a beautiful woman, somehow even more beautiful than the painting I was just admiring. Her paint-stained hands lead me to realize she must be the artist working on this piece—Jenna and Gabriella did tell me about this part of their wedding, but I wasn't paying much attention in all my prep for my performance.

"Sorry, could you move aside, please? I need to get back to it," the painter says, chuckling awkwardly.

Oops. I guess I was too busy staring to notice I was in the way.

"O-oh, sorry." I move aside so she can get back to the painting.

I try to step back enough so she doesn't feel crowded by my presence but I can't will myself to walk away completely. I want to see what she does next.

"You're welcome to stay and watch for a bit," she says, turning to me after filling in some of the clouds in the sky of the painting.

I clear my throat, realizing again that I've been mesmerized. Good art is just one of those things I could never look away from, but perhaps this is creepier than I mean it to be. My height makes me conscious that I can sometimes appear more intimidating than I am, especially to people who may not know me yet.

"Sure, sorry. I don't usually silently stand next to people I don't know but I couldn't help it. Your painting is beautiful," I say.

The artist smiles and I realize I want to write songs about that smile. A single dimple appears on her left cheek.

"Thank you. Your performance was quite good too... sorry, I forgot your name. Too many other details stored up here today." She taps the side of her head and giggles as she says the last part.

There's been a murder—death by giggles. *Relax, Brodie.* You've met pretty people before. You've sung in front of hundreds of people before. You can speak normally.

"It's Brodie," I say with a smile.

At least, I hope it's a smile and not a grimace as my hands begin to sweat from nervousness. No, it's the summer heat. It's just hot out.

"Nice to meet you, Brodie. I'm Taylor Evans. I'd shake your hand but mine is currently covered in paint."

I nod in understanding and Taylor smiles again before turning back to her work. I really should go get something to eat, but I also really want to watch this process. Maybe I should look up the artist on social media or something so I can find out more in a less creepy way.

I make it through three of the videos on her page (thank goodness her profile is under her name) before a tap on my arm interrupts me. I'm surprised to see Bea holding a plate with a fork in front of me.

"Here. You need to eat," she says, reaching for my phone.

I hastily put it in my pocket instead and grab the fork she's shoving in my face. I use my other hand to take the plate.

"Thank you. How did you know I haven't eaten yet?"

"Thank Steph," Bea says, gesturing to her girlfriend, who is still out on the dance floor. "She's been watching the portrait too, and she said it doesn't look like you took time between your set and now."

I don't bother correcting her assumption. Technically, I also had enough time to talk to the brides and contemplate my entire career as a singer. But Bea has heard enough of those musings, as we work together at the bookstore/café she manages, Love A Latte Books.

I dig into the food as Bea watches me, clearly not planning to leave until she's determined that I am sufficiently full.

Not wanting to just have her stare at me, I make some small talk.

"The ceremony was beautiful, right?"

"Yes," Bea says dreamily. "It was perfect. Honestly, this entire wedding is just a dream. Your performance too."

I shake my head but smile at the compliment. I'm out of practice, but I should take the crumbs of praise when I get them. It's not like anyone else will give them to me.

"Yes, the performance was amazing," Taylor chimes in from where she's refining the flowers in the arch depicted on the painting.

"See? Even the artist thinks so. Tell Brodie how amazing they are; they never believe it from me." Bea moves closer to the painter and introduces herself, while I keep eating and shaking my head.

I continue eating silently as they chat, thankfully away from the topic of me and now onto the topic of how talented Taylor is. It's a conversation I'd be happy to join but I decide to focus on eating, my empty stomach forcing me to pay attention to it now that I've finally stopped moving long enough to notice how starving I really was.

When I finish eating, I put the plate away on a nearby dirty dish tray and head back to Bea so we can continue our conversation.

"Well, I'll let you get back to it," Bea is saying to Taylor as she steps away upon my arrival.

Bea reaches for my arm and steers me away from the art station and towards the dance floor.

"C'mon, let's go dance our feet off." She drags me towards her girlfriend and the rest of the attendees.

Laughing, I join in the antics, and while my feet don't fall off at the end of the night, the smile on my face is one that will take several days to fade.

CHAPTER TWO

I wake up to the sound of my obnoxious ringtone, and I curse myself for not putting my phone on silent last night. It's not something I typically worry about, as I keep my notifications perpetually off for anything that isn't a call or text from my close friends. But now, I consider adding it to my list of things to do every night.

I've missed the call by the time I groggily crawl over towards my nightstand, where my phone is charging, but I jolt awake when I see that it was Jenna who called. As she's on her honeymoon in a remote cottage I don't even know where, there's no reason for her to be calling me.

I call her back immediately and she picks up after a few seconds.

"Hey, everything okay?" I ask, clearing my throat when the words get blocked by early morning grogginess.

"Yes, sorry for scaring you. What are you up to today?"

"Nothing, it's my day off. Why?"

"Can you do me a huge favour? Please, please," Jenna asks.

"Of course." I don't hesitate to accept.

Jenna is one of the few people I'd sacrifice a limb for if she asked, not that she would. There's a kinship we developed working in theatre together, and it's been easy to stay in touch with her, even now that the show is over. I've worked with and met lots of people in the entertainment business in my career but Jenna is one of the few pure-hearted ones, the kind who really look out for you. Being openly queer is also one of the things that made us click—not that a lot of people know much about my personal life. Jenna's one of the few people I feel comfortable talking with about all this and she's been a great shoulder to lean on as I figure my shit out. Not that there's much to figure out. I know who I am, but how or whether to tell other people is the part I struggle with.

"Can you pick up the portrait from the artist from our wedding today? Taylor Evans, did you meet her? She's heading out of town for a week and we don't come back until tomorrow. I know it's silly of me but I really want to come home to it. I'm too excited. Please?" Jenna continues as she tries to justify her request.

I shake my head, not that she can see it.

"It's not silly, of course I will. Just send me the details and I'll do it later today."

"Perfect, thank you! I'll text you the details. I'll call my building concierge to tell them too, so they'll let you in."

"Sure. . . so, how's the honeymoon?" I tease.

"Hmm? Oh, what's that, Gabriella? The breakfast is burning? Oh no!" Jenna's voice gets a bit distant as she starts to move the phone away from her ear.

"Stop with the theatrics, you actor." My laugh betrays me, as I can totally picture Jenna putting on this show. "Fine, I'll let you get back to whatever it is you're doing. I don't want to know. Bye," I say and hang up.

Well, at least that answers the question of what I was going to do today. The other option was to stare at my guitar and wait for a song to write itself. This is different from what I did yesterday, which was sitting at my laptop to wait for the Word document to fill itself with lyrics. The day before was similar, but with a notebook and a cup of coffee.

It's not that I don't want to write a new song, it's just that I *can't*. I haven't been able to for some time, which is why I continue to stay here in this city, while the world moves on and slowly forgets Quixotic. Maybe it's better this way, to fade into obscurity and live off the royalty cheques that come in as more and more of our songs go viral and are licensed for movies, TV shows, and car commercials.

But still, I want to write something. Anything. Just to prove to myself that I can do it. Maybe it's silly, but I'd feel more silly if I didn't at least try.

I take the subway to the address that Jenna sent me, already thinking about how I'll want to order a ride for the later trip to Jenna's. If I got any weird subway air or dirt on the painting, I'd probably fling myself onto the street before Jenna had a chance to. I'd never forgive myself.

Following the instructions Jenna texted me, I ring the doorbell and try not to get freaked out by the security camera attached to it.

"Hey, it's Brodie, here to pick up Jenna Daniels' painting," I say into the video doorbell.

A minute later, the door opens and Taylor waves me in.

"Hey, good to see you again," she says as I awkwardly stand in the front foyer.

"You too," I say, looking around.

There's no way to describe this house as being anything other than where an artist lives. The floor is covered in bright rugs; the walls have a mismatch of tapestries and paintings, some in Taylor's style and some in much more abstract ways; and even the furniture is unique. There are IKEA bookshelves, just like in every other Toronto home, but the tables and trinkets are all unique, at least from what I can see.

"Shoes on or off?" I finally remember to ask, now that I've been here for too long to just stand there. Even though Jenna told me this was the artist's studio, it still looks more like a home. I guess it's a home studio.

"Shoes off, please. I have the painting in the back, let me go grab it."

I kick my shoes off and hastily follow Taylor. "Oh no, let me. Please."

Taylor shrugs, allowing me to follow her deeper into the space.

Past the kitchen, which is fairly clear except for a monstrously high pile of dishes in the sink, is what would likely be a living room in anyone else's house. Here, it's clear that it's been transformed into a painting sanctuary.

The floor is covered in a white tarp like I've only ever seen in movies and there are empty white canvases stacked against the wall, next to a bookshelf that contains rows of paints, brushes, and a plethora of other artist tools.

In the centre of the room is the painting that I'm here to pick up, mounted on an easel.

"Here it is," says Taylor as she gestures to the centre of the room.

The moment is so cinematic that I ask Taylor if I can take a picture of the painting against this backdrop. Clearly used to this question, she agrees and lets me do my thing.

"Can I take one of you next to the painting as well? I think Jenna would like that," I add quickly at the end, wanting to make sure that my intentions are not misconstrued.

Not that I have any other intention, but you never know.

"Of course," Taylor says as she stands next to the painting.

I only take a few photos as Taylor smiles. She is really photogenic, but I don't tell her that. I don't want her to feel put out by the situation.

Taylor grabs the portrait and hands it to me, and I take it gently, as if my mere presence might somehow ruin the artwork. Maybe it can sense a lack of artistic talent; what if it spontaneously combusts?

"I put a protection polish over it so it should be fine against general dust, but try not to drop this outside," Taylor says.

My paranoia about that very thing happening must show on my face because she quickly adds, "Not that I think you would do that. I say that to everyone."

"Right. . . thank you. Can you just hold on to it for a second while I get my shoes and order my ride?"

"Sure, no problem."

Taylor diligently protects the painting while I do those things. I want to ask her about her career (How did she get started? Does she only do queer weddings? Was my performance at the wedding actually good?), but I decide to be reasonable and let those questions fade from my mind. I'm good at speaking to a crowd, a faceless blur of faces and people who don't really know me, other than as that singer from Quixotic, but as Brodie, as me, I don't know how to talk to people. Let alone a beautiful stranger who paints these precious moments, somehow more beautiful than her.

God, I can't say any of that. So I don't, and by the time I give it some more thought that night, I decide that I acted very normally earlier today and that is how I would prefer Taylor to remember me. That oddly polite friend of one of her clients; nothing more and nothing less.

The photo of the painting in her studio, and the one of her next to it, are well received by Jenna, who thanks me profusely for picking up the painting, later that night over text. She also appreciates the photo I took of the painting safely in her apartment, and I'm glad I had the foresight to do that. She sends another text,

> oh also, before I forget, here are some pictures my family sent me of your performance
>
> 12 images attached

> wow, these are high quality pics
>
> who took these?

> my cousin, she's a K-pop stan so she knows all the best angles to capture any performance

> wow, please thank her for me. Is it okay if I post this on insta?

> yeah I'm sure she'd love it. Please also send me that selfie we took together, I want to add it to my wedding album

> 4 images attached

> not sure which one you're talking about so take them all, I'll post the one that I look the best in on mine

> of course, my liege, enjoy

> okay stop texting me and go back to your wife, let's catch up when you're back and settled

> oh you're right. . . my wife 😌

> bye 😌

    I stay true to my word and go to post the best selfie of the three of us, as well as the other pics of me that Jenna's cousin took. I know the internet has already exploded a little over Jenna's wedding (I ignore the notifications but it's not like I don't see them when I open my apps) and I'm sure these photos will only add to that. Anything to help Gabriella's dream of being able to retire from the tech industry so she can live in service of Jenna's every whim; a dream I am more than happy to support.

    At the end of the image carousel, I decide to add the picture of the portrait in Taylor's studio. It's a beautiful photo, with the portrait set against such a quintessential artist's dream studio. The photo was captured at a decent distance, so that some of the details of the portrait are fuzzy enough that it looks ethereal in the afternoon sunlight that pours in across it. I tag Taylor's studio account in the photo too (a fellow artist has to credit another!) and I caption the post with: 'Outtakes from the wedding of two of my favourite people. Love you, J & G.'

It doesn't take long for the comments to flood in, and this late at night, my usual defences against the internet are severely lowered. I read a few nice ones before deciding this can't last forever so I close it out. I heart the ones I do see, though.

music4ever: okay brodie comeback when ???

shelsie879: wow that painting

ingrid.gordon: omg friendship goals

Before I can get too deep into the endless scrolling, I fling my phone across the room and grab the latest Ocean Vuong book from my nightstand instead. I read a few more pages before my eyes close on their own, already forgetting about the internet chatter about my life.

CHAPTER THREE

A week later, I've forgotten all about the post and the post-wedding antics. The day starts the same as always, with Bea asking about my regular day off as she enters the bar area, where I'm washing some of the cups left behind by the morning regulars.

"It was nice, I had a chance to relax."

"Great, that's exactly what you needed." She claps me on the shoulder as she turns back towards the ordering station.

Our usual weekday lunchtime is slow, as our café really only serves drinks and the occasional cookie, which are all sold out by this time. This is my favourite time of day, though, a time to relax and yap with Bea for an hour or two before my shift ends because of the early morning start.

Halfway through our gossip session, a customer walks up, interrupting us. It's not any customer, though. As if materializing from my imagination, Taylor Evans walks in. Her hair is tied up and she has a pair of silver-framed glasses on. This casual side to her is so different from the formal side I saw at the wedding, and the artsy painter I saw last week. Oh my God, I'd better not be blushing.

"Hey, Bea. Hi, Brodie," she says, smiling.

"Oh my gosh, you actually came!" Bea exclaims excitedly.

"Well, I was promised free coffee." She's still smiling and I try to memorize the image while I can.

"Okay, the city's best oat milk hazelnut iced latte, coming right up," Bea says and turns around to make it.

"How's your day going?" Taylor asks me now that we're sort of alone; the machine whirring behind me indicates that Bea is too in the zone to really pay attention.

"G-good," I manage to get out, hoping I sound normal.

"That's. . . good," Taylor responds.

Bea places the cup on the counter with a light clink.

"Ta-da! Please let me know what you think."

"Of course." Taylor grabs the cup and takes a sip. She nods appreciatively and smiles at Bea. "Very delicious, thank you."

"You're welcome." My boss beams.

This is just Bea's generous, warm nature, but if this was anyone else, I'd likely have glared at them in jealousy for flirting with Taylor. Not that there's anything to be jealous over, it's just that. . . Well. I like to keep my crushes mine. How else would I be able to write all those songs that the BookTok creators use for their videos about books with possessive love interests? Not that I've publicly admitted to having seen those videos; they just occasionally come across my feed and then the books make their way to my e-reader.

"Brodie, do you have a moment to chat later?" Taylor surprises me by asking.

Me?

"Of course they do. Their shift ends in thirty," Bea helpfully answers for me.

"Great, I'll just grab a seat. Come find me when you're ready, no rush at all." Taylor waves goodbye as she walks over towards the art section.

She's already gone by the time my arm is up in a responding wave, and I awkwardly lower it before another customer can see my idiocy.

Bea elbows me, my faux pas not going completely unnoticed.

"You okay there, bud?"

"Yes, why wouldn't I be?" Now if only I could speak so coherently in front of Taylor, then I'd really be set.

"If you say so... I can't wait to find out what she wants to talk to you about." Bea winks at me and I lightly swat my dish towel at her.

"As if I'd tell you, blabbermouth."

"Yeah, right. Now, tell me, what was last week's post about? All the gossip blogs have already written all about Brodie's first post in months, a comeback in the works. It's the only thing I've been seeing for the past week. Taylor turning up reminded me of her portrait too."

"There's nothing to it, other than the fact that two of my favourite people got married."

Bea nods in understanding. "That was a great wedding, huh?"

Luckily, the rest of my shift passes by in a blur, thanks to my easy conversation with Bea about the wedding (we both love love!), so by the time I have my apron off and tote bag on, I'm feeling relaxed. This will just be a simple conversation. Maybe Taylor wants an autograph; stranger things have happened.

I clear my throat as I approach the table where she's sitting, her cup now empty and her head in a book. While the cover has a fairly innocuous illustration, I've read it and know that the contents are smuttier than even I expected. I almost want to tell her that I enjoyed the book before I remember I'm in public and anyone could hear; the last thing I'd want the fan blogs to report on is my reading habits.

"Hey, Taylor," I settle on.

"Oh, hey, Brodie." She places a paper bookmark in the book and throws it into her bag. "Take a seat," she says and gestures to the empty one in front of her.

I nod and sit down, folding my legs beneath the chair carefully so they don't accidentally kick her. My long legs have gotten me in trouble before; usually by tripping over things, so I wouldn't put it past them to kick the most beautiful person here.

"Thank you for tagging me in your post last week. I was away for a destination wedding for the past few days and I came back to so many new followers and even more inquiries through my website," she says, sounding sincerely grateful.

"You're very welcome," I respond, waving a hand as if to brush off the thanks.

"What are you doing after this?"

"N-nothing. Just going to go home and have lunch. Why?"

"Why don't we get lunch together? My treat, as a thank you," Taylor offers.

With her brown eyes on me and that irresistible smile, I can only agree.

Now, sitting in front of each other at the all-you-can-eat sushi restaurant, I have to admit I was probably hungrier than I thought. And this restaurant has been on my to-go list for a while now, thanks to all the food recommendation videos Steph sends me. I'll have to report back to her on whether the salmon sushi pizza is as good as the videos make it out to be.

So far, the conversation between us has flowed smoothly, mainly just me asking Taylor all the questions I had about her painting process that I was holding back last time we spoke.

But just as I'm now more comfortably shoving dragon rolls into my mouth, her next sentence takes me by surprise: "I actually have an ulterior motive for inviting you here."

I chew slowly and make sure to swallow properly so I don't choke. "Pardon me?"

"I mean, I was hoping to ask you for a favour." Taylor laughs, and if I didn't know any better, I'd think that she was blushing a little bit.

"What is it?"

"If it's okay with you, can I paint you sometime?"

"Me?"

"Yes, you." She laughs again, as if me finding the question ridiculous is, well, ridiculous. Oops, I didn't mean to say that aloud.

"Even expert painters need to practise, to hone their skills," she starts to explain, "and I've been wanting to find someone interesting to paint. I want to get better at solo portraits, not just wedding photos. Not that I dislike doing those, but I want to try doing more than one thing so I have a wider range of options to offer my clients. Y'know?"

I nod because I know that feeling too well.

"I know people say that it's good to have your niche, but as an artist, I could never really understand that. It's always good to experiment, to try new things," I say and Taylor nods.

"Exactly. It's good that I have something I'm known for but I want to try this too. I've had enough practice painting and sketching actors and 2D characters, so now I want to try painting a live person."

I nod.

"So, you'll do it, right?" she asks, hopefully.

I take a minute to think about it. It's not as if I have anything better to do, and as a fellow artist, I have to help her out. Who knows? Maybe the experience will finally inspire some new music or at least the beginning of a song.

"Sure, why not?"

"Oh my gosh, thank you so much," Taylor practically shrieks, grabbing my hands in delight. "Thank you, thank you. You won't regret it." She continues to shake my hands up and down.

All I can do is shake my head at her delight and hope the smile on my face doesn't show how secretly excited I am.

Later that night, a melody appears in my head. The moment happens so fleetingly that I almost miss the opportunity to grab my guitar. I hum a little as I work it out, and while it's not quite there, I can tell it's the start of something.

I'm practically floating on cloud nine as I wander around my apartment afterwards, hoping to get out some of my excited energy. I could try to work more on the song but I know enough about my creative process that this feeling of excitement is helpful only in marketing, and not in creating. Creating like this makes the music frantic, jumping from place to place as my thoughts jumble in excitement. Other artists probably have a different method but I need complete calm to write. It's likely why I haven't been able to write anything in so long; it's been a while since I felt completely at peace.

Pacing isn't enough; I need to talk to someone. Not wanting to bother my Toronto besties, I decide to check on the semi-neglected group chat I have with the other Quixotic members. It's not that I'm ignoring them on purpose; it's just that, while they're all happily doing their own thing in their home states, I've been here trying to figure out how to tell them that the boy band the internet is obsessed with isn't all boys, not really.

<gif of someone poking their head in>

TRAVIS
omg bro is that you

TRAVIS
who hacked Brodie's phone?

TRAVIS
RJ was it you

RJ
nah man I'm not even in canada rn

RJ
jones?

JONES
sorry I'm busy rn, trying to find the bodysnatchers that took our boy brodie

A slight ping of nerves hits my stomach at their usual guy talk and I grit through it, trying to tell myself that this is a product of my own doing.

no bodysnatchers here, just missed my boys

This part is true. For all the shit they give me about not checking in more often, they are generally supportive of everything I do. Travis came to see me on Broadway a year ago, and RJ and Jones sent flowers. When I moved to Toronto, RJ flew in to help me with the move, claiming that he had to come to town to visit his family. I know his family is actually in Calgary, completely on the other side of the country. They donate to charities as often as I do and don't hesitate to hold up rainbow flags at our concerts, getting us ruled out of eligibility for large music festivals abroad. The memories come flooding all at once and I have to remember that it is physically impossible for me to actually kick myself for being so stupid as to not talk to them sooner.

> RJ
> wow 😢 I miss you too bud
>
> JONES
> yeah, it's been too long

My phone soon flashes with the words, *INCOMING CALL FROM TRAVIS TO QUIXOTIC 4EVER CHAT.*

Smiling, I pick up the phone and join the group call.

"Figured this was easier than texting," Travis says as we all join the call and say our hellos.

"Way easier," RJ chimes in, his melodic voice immediately recognizable.

"So, Brodie, what's with the sudden sentiment? You doing okay?" Jones asks, always the straight shooter.

"Yes, I'm doing good. Still figuring my shit out but getting there, I think. I started working on a new song today," I rush out, my earlier excitement about actually writing something coming forth.

"Woah, that's great!" Travis says, clearly excited.

I blush as more cheers come through from everyone else too.

"Enough, enough, it's no big deal," I say to stop the onslaught of compliments that get more and more unhinged as my bandmates go on.

Being called "the world's greatest singer/songwriter" is definitely a reach—especially coming from Travis, who has written most of our greatest hits himself.

"Speaking of no big deal, what's with the insta post?" RJ continues.

"What do you mean?" I ask, genuinely confused.

"You know, the one of the art. You even tagged the very pretty artist. Don't think we wouldn't find out, especially with the fan theories everywhere."

"As far as soft launches go, it's a pretty good one," Jones chimes in.

"First of all, there's nothing to tell or report because there was no hidden meaning to it, other than wanting to uplift the work of a fellow creative person. Anything to help a fellow artist, y'know?"

Snickers come from all three of my bandmates.

"Dude, we know you." Travis stops giggling long enough to try an actual rebuttal of the obvious truth. "You only post serious shit, and whatever our old label told us you had to. You only post something if it seriously impacted you. There's no point to it otherwise, as you were so fond of telling us when we posted too many thirst traps."

Jones doesn't hesitate to respond to the side dig. "In my defence, the thirst traps are very necessary for my mental health. I need external validation to go on stage."

I roll my eyes, as I'm sure everyone else on the call is doing as well.

"Chill, there's nothing to it, other than what I already said," I say again, hoping that nonchalance (and a lack of being able to see my face) will help.

They're not right about the photo, but they're not exactly wrong either. How do I tell them that seeing the painting in such a picturesque setting inspired a calmness that I hadn't felt in quite some time? That the artwork reminded me how extraordinary creative people are?

I definitely can't tell them about the portrait session I have with Taylor later this week, or that we had lunch together today.

"Okay, if you say so," RJ acquiesces, being his usual agreeable self.

Phew. I manage to ask the guys questions about how they're doing, how their work is going, and find out a bit more about what Travis has been up to in Hollywood. It's his first major acting role, playing the bad boy love interest in a movie by a new production company.

The call lasts way longer than I anticipated it would, and by the end, I'm curled up on my couch, stifling a yawn. That doesn't stop the huge smile on my face, and when the call ends, I don't hesitate to tell them that I love them, as I always do when we talk.

"We have to do this again sometime," Travis says and we all agree before hanging up.

Now that my nerves are settled a bit (what am I? An old Victorian maid?), I reach for my notebook and jot some lyrics. As with the melody that came earlier, I'm not sure whether these will ever see the light of day but I'm happy to have at least done something.

CHAPTER FOUR

A few days later, on my next day off, I stand in front of Taylor's studio, working up the courage to ring the doorbell. I don't want to be late so I should get to it sooner rather than later, but for now, I'm going to wallow in my nervousness.

You can do this, Brodie. You've sung in front of thousands of people before. This is just one painting.

But thousands of concertgoers don't get to talk to you the same way an artist would. Dissect every out-of-place hair and awkward clothes. Did I wear the right outfit? I just chose a simple black T-shirt and slightly baggy jeans. Should I have worn something that gives singer energy? I don't even know what that would be. I smooth the ends of my hair nervously before taking a deep breath.

Okay, here goes nothing.

I ring the doorbell and Taylor opens the door a minute later. Kicking off my shoes inside, I follow her to the studio. We exchange the usual pleasantries, and if she can tell I'm being extra short today because of my nervousness, she doesn't say so.

Inside the studio, Taylor has set up a canvas to the side, with a stool in the centre of the room. Thank goodness I've been told I have good posture; otherwise, I'd be worried about how hunched over I'd look sitting in a chair with no back support.

"Why don't you sit down while I pick out the paints?" Taylor asks, gesturing towards the middle of the room.

I nod and take my seat, leaving my tote bag in the corner of the room, away from the chair.

I brought a book with me to read but I'm not quite sure how this works. I imagine I can't do anything other than just sit here, so I just watch as Taylor fusses around the room, grabbing different colour paints and various paintbrushes. She spends an extra few minutes on the blue, perhaps trying to find the right colour for my jeans? I want to ask but my nervousness combined with my curiosity is keeping me silent, lest I inadvertently ruin the experience.

"I think I've got what I need," Taylor says as she sits at the chair behind her easel.

With the way her chair is set up at an angle, she can turn towards me and her painting at the same time. I watch as she starts mixing paints together on what I can only describe as a stone slab. She glances between me and the paints every few seconds, and I try to make sure to keep my face neutral. I guess, if this is the view I'll get for the next few hours, there could be much worse ways to spend the day.

When she's done mixing the paints, she puts down the marble slab on a short table that rests on the other side of the easel furthest away from me.

She stares at me for a minute or two, as if studying every detail about me. It's strange, being watched in this way and I realize this must be how every bowl of fruit that has ever been painted must feel. Strangely, the feeling isn't all that weird. It's how stylists and photographers watch you on set, trying to figure out which detail is out of place or won't align with their vision. Except I'm not quite sure if there's a vision to this today. I feel as if I'm being studied as Brodie the person not Brodie the artist and I don't know how to grapple with that feeling.

SONG FOR YOU

After a few more minutes, in which Taylor also grabs a sketchbook and starts sketching something on the page, the only sound that fills the room is the sound of graphite on paper.

What do people usually think about in these situations? Should I make a joke? If I start thinking any more about myself, I fear I may need to hide for a week.

"Should I put on some music?" Taylor asks, as if sensing that my thought spiral was close to reaching its end.

I nod and Taylor connects her phone to a Bluetooth speaker that I didn't notice before. Jazz fills the air and I smile at the song choice. I quietly hum as Taylor continues sketching, and when the song changes, she smiles at me.

"You can sing if you want," she says.

"No thanks," I immediately reply.

"Why not? I'll sing with you. This can just be for fun," she says and then she starts to join the singer in their melody.

Except, well, she's a horrible singer. She must know it because she laughs at the look on my face and keeps singing, quieter this time, as she moves her pencil from her sketchbook to the canvas in front of her. I join her at the chorus and she smiles wide as I tap my thighs lightly to the beat.

"See? That wasn't so bad," she says when the song ends.

"I was doing just fine. You, on the other hand. . ." I trail off, hoping she takes it as the joke it's meant to be.

"I know, I'm not the best singer. But think about it. Imagine if I could paint like this and sing? I'd be unstoppable. I need one fatal flaw to keep me humble."

I laugh and shake my head as she gets back to her sketching. Not wanting to distract her too much, I continue to hum softly for a bit in time with the music, not bothering to wipe the smile off my face.

After a bit, she asks me if I'd like a bit of a break, so I stand up to stretch my legs and she hands me a glass of water as well.

"Thank you," I say, gratefully.

"Of course. Let me know if you need anything else. The artist is only as good as their subject, so your comfort matters to me."

"Well, thank you."

After I finish the water, I hand the glass back to Taylor. She takes it but continues to stand in front of me, head tilted. I want to ask if there's anything else but her question interrupts me.

"Have you ever tied up your hair?"

"No... why?"

"I think it'd look nice. Do you mind?"

I nod so she puts down the glass and grabs an elastic that was on her wrist. She gently grabs my arm, leading me to sit back on the stool.

Now standing behind me, she gently takes my hair and ties it at the base of my neck. Her fingers smooth out the strands as she works and I hope the blush I feel coming on doesn't show on the back of my neck. This must be what romance novels talk about when they say how intimate it is to have someone tie your hair for you. I get it now.

When she's done, she moves to stand in front of me. If she's aware of how close she is, she doesn't seem awkward or fazed by it. She continues to study my face, as if committing it to memory, and with this opportunity, I decide to do the same.

Up close, her beauty stuns me. I wonder what she thinks of me. I steal a glance at her lips and my heart quickens with the thought of how soft they must be. I have to remind myself that, if she's doing the same, it must only be because she needs to paint me.

Is she imagining what would happen if she took a step closer? Perhaps stood in between my legs, letting me kiss my way down her collarbone, exposed by the scoop-neck T-shirt she's wearing.

She takes a step back and I swallow down the thought, trying not to clear my throat, which feels stuck with the things I'm trying not to say.

"Yes, the tied-up hair was the right choice. You look so pretty," she says softly, as if unsure.

I flush again at the compliment. I've been called many things before but *pretty* is a new one, and I like it more than I thought I would.

Taylor returns to her canvas and I'm grateful there's music playing so I can try to focus on that and not the hearts that must be visible floating around my head.

After another hour or two—I'm not quite sure exactly how long—Taylor proposes a break for lunch. While she makes a salad (after assuring me it will be worth the wait), I wander around her studio to stretch my legs and admire the paintings. While there are some wedding paintings in progress and a large corkboard with various thank you notes and postcards, there are also some other pieces hidden around. A splatter painting here, a large landscape of the setting sun against a cozy cabin there. Everything she paints seems to have this magic sparkle, a certain je ne sais quoi to it that leaves me in wonder.

"Bon appetite!" Taylor yells from the kitchen and I chuckle and walk over to the bar seating that's opposite her kitchen island. She stands as she eats and I do the same, knowing that I'll be sitting for a while again afterwards.

"The painting is coming along nicely," I tell her.

I got a glimpse on my way across the room and it looks like she's finished the outline and larger shapes and is beginning to fill in the details of my face. My facial features remain unfinished; blank eyes and only an outline for my mouth and nose, which was a bit eerie to see, but my hair in a ponytail looked pretty good. I'll have to check it in the washroom later to see if it's just painter's magic or not.

"Thank you, but I think it'll still take a few more hours. I'll probably do another hour or two today and then let you go. I can just take a picture to finish out your face and the background later. I'm using oil paints so it'll take a few layers anyway."

"Cool." I nod as I finally take a bit of the salad.

She was right; it's surprisingly good. The inclusion of tangerines with a light balsamic sauce feels fancier than anything I'd ever make for myself.

"Good, right?" Taylor asks as I keep eating.

I was perhaps hungrier than I thought. I take the opportunity to ask Taylor some more questions about her business and the logistics of how it works. She gives me the details, and while such a detailed explanation for something that may seem a bit mundane might normally bore me, I'm fascinated by the way she lights up, even in describing how annoying it is to transport all her painting equipment to wedding locations. It sounds like a lot more work than I anticipated, and I'm in awe of how much of a business person she must be to have successfully become a full-time artist. Most days, I feel like I've lucked into my success and she has clearly worked hard for hers.

"Sorry, is this boring?" she asks, glancing anxiously at my salad bowl, as she seems to have noticed I've finished most of my salad, while hers remains only a quarter eaten.

"Not at all, it's interesting. You clearly love what you do." I hope my smile comes across as the genuine one I mean for it to be.

"I do, not that it's not hard work but I find it rewarding. And I get to meet cool people, and especially cool people in love. That's always nice. . ." She trails off for a bit before turning back to me. "What about you, don't you love what you do? You're pretty famous, from what I've seen online. Not that I've googled you. Okay, maybe I did. But I mean—"

I interrupt her before she has a chance to continue; a fellow nervous rambler can recognize another and help them end their internal misery. "I wouldn't say I'm that famous. I'm more famous in the States than here, so being here is almost like a vacation. It only appears like that when you google me. . . and yes, I do love it. I love my bandmates and the feeling of being on a stage, performing for people. It's just that, to be a self-producing band, you have to keep producing music, and well, it's been some time since I've written anything new."

She hums in sympathy. "It can be hard when you need to keep

producing creative ideas. At least my business is pretty self-sustaining, since I rely on other people, not myself, for ideas."

"That's true. I'm just trying to do a bit of reading, walking around, exploring the city. I'm hoping something will inspire me."

"I hope so too, because I really like your music."

I laugh at that and wave my hand in a dismissive gesture. "You don't have to pretend to for my sake."

"No, no, I really do. I've been a fan of Quixotic for a while, but in the way where I have all your music downloaded and know nothing about the group. I find that's better for me; I've always felt weird about being too into a music group. They're people outside of their work, y'know?"

"Okay, I get it. You're one of those 'I knew them before they got cool' people," I tease, hoping she takes it as the joke it is.

Taylor giggles and sticks her tongue out. "And so what if I am?"

I shake my head, finishing up the last bite of the food.

I wait for Taylor to finish her bowl, and when she does, I stand to get the plates to walk them over to the sink but she beats me to it. When she turns back around, she has a more serious look on her face.

"Do you mind if I ask you something?"

The question of whether it is okay to be questioned always leaves me with a bit of nerves but I'm working on opening up to people, so I nod.

"Forgive me if this is a bit rude, but I noticed that all your promo content, or really any article about Quixotic misgenders you. Have you not 'come out'?"

She gestures air quotes for the last part, as if she's not sure how exactly to phrase what she means.

"I don't mind, I just don't speak to a lot of people about it. I haven't really addressed it. I guess it's just a bit new to me."

"That's fair. The internal realization is sometimes the hardest part. That was how I felt when I realized I was bisexual."

"Thanks," I say with sincerity. Not that I expected her to be unaccepting, but it is always nice to hear that someone can relate even just a little bit. "This is probably awkward to say but I'd appreciate it if you didn't say anything, I mean, I don't know if I'm ready to start putting out press releases about it. I have to tell the rest of the guys first. And I really want to write a new song first."

"Do you think a new song will help them take the news well?"

That's an abrupt question, but it's surprisingly insightful and I think it over. "I guess the song isn't really for them. It's for me. I think I somehow want to prove to myself that I can still be *me*, even if the way I feel about myself has changed. Well, the way I feel about myself hasn't actually changed. I guess I just have the words now to tell people that how they should see me is how I see myself. I don't know... gahh." I trail off, not wanting to turn this lunch break into my own personal gender theory discussion.

Taylor comes around to my side of the island and puts a comforting hand on my shoulder.

"It's okay not to know everything. Thank you for sharing with me."

I smile at that and have to resist the urge to grab her hand and keep it on my shoulder when she lets go after a few more gentle pats.

"And for what it's worth, I think your new music will be even better. I can't wait to hear it."

"You and me both."

CHAPTER FIVE

It takes two weeks for the new song to be done. It's not perfect; heck, it's probably unperformable but it's complete and it has words and a melody. Normally, at this phase of the process, I'd send it to Travis but I'm hesitant to do so. Maybe my desire to have the band see the best in me is related to my fear of wanting to come out to them only in the perfect way, in a way to show them and the world that I'm the same Brodie they know and love. Maybe even better.

I consider sharing it with Bea or Jenna but their opinion means too much to me, and I don't want to show them this messy part of my process. But another artist would understand...

And that's how I've convinced myself it would totally be appropriate to share this song with Taylor, of all people.

We haven't talked much since I left the studio, but that's because I don't quite know how to talk to her without ending it in a string of compliments that would seem out of place coming from someone she just met. At least with the song, I'm just asking for a return on the favour I did by letting her paint me.

> hey hope you're doing well

hey yes I am. hope you are too

Whether or not she's weirded out by the strangely formal greeting, she doesn't say so. Meanwhile, I'm kicking myself because, seriously, what is this? A work email?

if you have some time over next few days, I was hoping you'd be free to listen and give me some feedback on a new song

as one artist to another, in return for the portrait

omg of course I'd be happy to

the weather on the weekend looks to be nice, I was thinking of going to trinity bellwoods for a picnic & sketch session. Want to join me with your guitar?

I work on sunday but I can do saturday, that sounds nice

let's meet at 11 outside the park entrance, I'll bring the blanket & snacks

no no let me bring some snacks too, any requests?

some gummy bears and miss vickie's salt & vinegar chips

done, but don't those chips burn your mouth too much?? I can only eat a few

nope, I happen to have a very sturdy mouth I'll have you know

never mind, just buy a bag of all dressed ruffle chips as backup

> okay will do, I haven't tried all dressed chips yet

WHAT

those are a national canadian treasure

how have you been living here for a while and you haven't tried those

> idk I'm not a chip person 🌽

this is a crime, we'll fix this on saturday

> I'll see you then 😊
>
> can't wait

Before I have time to beat myself up for perhaps being too forward with my last text, Taylor hearts the message and I have to stop myself from skipping around the apartment. It's fine, I can be chill.

On Saturday, I end up arriving early at the park, overestimating how long it would take to pick up some snacks before walking over there. With my guitar case on my back, I'm a bit more paranoid than usual about people recognizing me, but with my baseball cap on, most people give me a wide berth. My height is an advantage, as with my head down, someone would really have to be in my space to recognize my face.

At 11:01, I put my phone back in my pocket and look around, spotting Taylor waiting to cross the street towards the park entrance. She catches my eye immediately and she waves to me from her side of the street. With a polka dot sundress on and her hair tied up, she looks positively radiant. She has a backpack on and a tote bag that looks much too large for her, and when she reaches me, I immediately tug the tote bag off her shoulder and insist on carrying it.

She talks my ear off about how annoying her commute was as we walk into the park and I listen to the chatter absentmindedly, more nervous about what she'll think of my song, now that the time to share it has arrived.

Miraculously, we find an empty spot where we can sit under a large tree and Taylor takes a picnic blanket from the tote bag I'm carrying and rolls it out. She drops her backpack and opens it, taking out her sketchbook and a cute transparent pencil case.

I sit down next to her and turn to her with a smile on my face. "Is this the part of the picnic where I ask you to paint me like one of your French girls?" I ask.

She swats my arm and laughs loud enough that a couple a few trees away turns to look at us.

"How long have you been holding that one in?"

"For two weeks. I kind of regretted not having the confidence to say it when I was at your studio a few weeks ago."

"You're ridiculous," she says but she's smiling. "So, let's hear this new song." She claps her hands together in eager anticipation.

"Right now? Let a person get comfortable," I say, shaking out my hands nervously.

Taylor grabs my right hand, stopping the nervousness.

"It's okay. A first draft doesn't have to be perfect. You can always make tweaks," she says, squeezing my hand for emphasis.

"R-right." I try to nod calmly, my brain short-circuiting at all that has already happened this afternoon.

I detach myself from her hand so I can open my guitar case. I rest the guitar on my lap and take a deep breath.

Taking a quick glance around, no one around us seems to be paying any attention. We've managed to sit down far enough away from the main pathway that strangers wouldn't pass by here and the couples and groups of friends around us seem to be too engaged in their own thing.

"You got this," Taylor whispers, staring intently at me.

Thinking the silent wish I say to myself every time before a show, I take a deep breath and start playing. It's hard for me to make eye contact with Taylor, so I focus on the trees around us and the wonderful scenery. When I do look at Taylor, I have to stop myself from smiling.

"Wow, that was amazing." Taylor claps when I finish the song.

I blush and put my guitar down next to me. "Thank you, but I think you're just saying that."

"No, I mean it!" she insists.

"What did you think of the words? Anything that I need to change?" I ask as I reach into my guitar case to grab my notebook.

I already have an idea of what doesn't quite click but I'm not sure what would work better, so I spend a few minutes running Taylor through my ideas.

"Hmm, maybe you can end the sentence here, and move this verse to the end instead. This word doesn't rhyme with that one the same way."

Even though she's not a singer, she's surprisingly creative and I jot down all her ideas. I'll still have to practise the tweaks but I think I'm much closer to sharing it with the group than I was before.

"Thank you I really appreciate it," I say gratefully, throwing my notebook down in the universal gesture of 'I need to take a break.'

Taylor nods and reaches into her tote bag, taking out a bag of candy.

"What's that?" I ask.

"Just all the Canadian snacks I could think of forcing you to try. That's how you can repay me," she says.

She reaches into the bag and passes me a yellow-wrapped chocolate bar. "Here, start with a Coffee Crisp."

"I've had these before." I smile as I open the candy and eat it anyway.

We spend the next few minutes stuffing our faces with snacks until we both can't possibly imagine eating another piece of candy.

Taylor dramatically flops to the ground in defeat after she finishes off the last of the Miss Vickie's chips.

"How am I supposed to get back to drawing now? I'm in a food coma," she groans, rubbing her stomach.

I'm sure I'm not supposed to find this as endearing as I do.

I pat her stomach sympathetically, "There, there," I say.

She shakes her head and sits up so her back is facing me. She scoots backwards until she's now leaning against my side.

"What if I just lean on you while I draw?"

"You can try but that probably won't work from the side. You should probably draw from here," I say and pat the space between my legs.

I've only seen this pose in photoshoots and move posters but it should work, as I am quite large compared to her.

Taylor nods gratefully and stands up so she can sit back down between my legs. She grabs her sketchbook and leans against me, the feel of her back warm against my chest.

Thank goodness she can't see the expression on my face, because I'm sure I'm blushing up a storm.

Because of my height, I can still see over Taylor's shoulder towards what she's sketching. She's drawing my guitar resting against the picnic blanket and I'm mesmerized by the way her hands move, shading the light as it hits the guitar perfectly.

She interrupts my reverie. "I'd ask you to play your guitar for me but I'm too comfortable right now."

"That's okay, I'm happy to watch you draw. I really wish I could do it."

"You can. There's no time like the present to start."

Before I can ask what she means, she grabs my hand and curls her pencil around it.

She guides my hand across the page,

"Not too much pressure there," she chides as I try to mimic the shading she was doing.

Her smaller hand guiding mine shouldn't be as thrilling as it is, but I find myself unable to say anything and just listen to her notes.

When I seem to have done it correctly, she praises me with an extra pat to the hand and a, "Good job, angel," and if it was physically possible, I would melt into a puddle right behind her.

She continues guiding me through the sketches for a few more minutes until I release the pencil and hand it back to her.

"I think that's enough for me. I'd rather watch you draw. You're more talented than me."

"Still, we all have to start somewhere," she says, turning back around to smile at me.

I smile wide when I notice that her face is flushed, but I don't comment on it. If I acknowledge it, maybe it'd ruin this little bubble of peace we've created.

CHAPTER SIX

My phone pings with a text from RJ.

> yo brodie
>
> what's with the PDA?
>
> <link>

I wasn't expecting the first thing I see when I woke up this morning to be a video of me with Taylor in the park, that's for sure.

The video is short, only 10-15 seconds, and it shows a group of people holding up a book before it cuts to a zoomed-in shot of me singing to Taylor. Thankfully, the video is using the latest Quixotic song that went viral for sound, so my singing isn't audible, but the caption reads: "POV: you go to book club in the park and see your favourite singer serenading his girlfriend."

The statement is false, on both accounts, but I feel like such an idiot. The video has over a million likes and I can already picture the headlines on *TMZ* and our fan blogs rolling in. I scroll through the comments, wanting to prepare myself for what I will see. . .

"Omg that is so cute"

"how does it feel to be living my dream"

"if you zoom in you can see me in the background running into traffic"

While the statements are all pretty generic so far, there is no doubt in my mind that it won't take long for people to speculate about who is in the video, especially because of my last Instagram post.

> thanks for bringing this to my attention man
>
> guess I'll have to call Seoyun

At least RJ texted me privately, and now I can take care of this before I have to start getting ready for my afternoon café shift. I pick up the phone and dial Seoyun, Quixotic's saviour and literal angel.

I flush as I remember how Taylor called me that yesterday. *Focus, Brodie, focus.* You have bigger fish to fry.

The line rings for a while but she picks up just before the call is set to go to voicemail.

"Seoyun speaking."

"Hey, it's Brodie."

"Hey!" Her voice seems to warm up on the phone.

"Did you not save my number?"

"This is a Canadian number, why would I have it saved? To be honest, I'm surprised to hear from you. I thought I wasn't allowed to bother you until you had a new song to share with me. Boss's orders," she teases, reminding me that I call her the actual boss of our little label, though on paper, it's me.

"Right. I'm not calling you about that. I'm calling because a video of me went viral."

"Oooh, is it one of those thirst trap edits? While that's great news, I'm not sure it merits a call."

Even in the most stressful of times, Seoyun knows exactly how to make me crack up and I laugh.

"It's not one of those. Hold on, I'll just send it to you," I say, pasting the link to the video into a new text to Seoyun. The line goes quiet for a few seconds as she watches it.

"I mean, the video isn't so damaging, but I can see why you'd be concerned. Do you want to put out a statement?"

"That's why I need your help. I'm sure some press will be calling you soon for a comment. Can you just clarify that I don't have a girlfriend?"

"Of course. What wording should we use?"

"Close friend is fine."

Seoyun makes a sound of affirmation, and despite the nervousness in my stomach, I decide to tell her about the rest of the statement too.

"S-Seoyun, I need you to do something else for me too."

Seoyun's easy tone turns more serious. "Of course. What is it?"

"In the statements, could you avoid using gendered words for me? I mean... my pronouns are they/them now."

"Okay, sure. I can do that."

I let out a deep breath, grateful that she didn't ask anything else about it.

"Do you want to put out a statement about that?" she asks, her tone not so much in interrogation mode but rather I-need-to-get-this-right-for-my-client mode.

"No, not yet. I'm still figuring that out. I'll do something myself when I'm ready. For now, though, let's just clarify the girlfriend rumours if anyone calls you about it."

"Sounds good. Do you want to talk about your next album?"

Before I can even attempt to answer that question, Seoyun curses.

"Let's talk later. I already have a call from someone at *Entertainment Weekly*. I have to get this."

Seoyun hangs up before I can respond either way, but I don't take offence at it. This is the nature of her job and why we pay her a generous portion of our royalties. She keeps things running so she can handle PR stuff like this, while I have the important job of writing new music. When I actually can.

Before I can chicken out of it, I call Taylor next.

"Hello?"

"Hey, it's Brodie," I say.

"Yes, I know," she laughs. "I have caller ID."

"Right. Right."

"What's up?"

"I just wanted to give you a head's up that there's a video of us in the park from yesterday that went viral. Not sure if that's the only one or if there's more, but I wanted to let you know that my team is on it. We won't name you or anything."

"Oh. Huh," Taylor responds.

I stay silent to give her some time to process it, not wanting to push her.

"Well, going viral isn't too bad. It's happened a few times with my videos as it is," she finally says.

"I know, but that's about your work, not about you," I respond gently. "It's a whole different circus when people are making comments about the quality of your character rather than your work."

"Right."

"If it helps, I've asked my team to clarify that we're just close friends."

Taylor laughs. "*Your team* sounds so fancy."

I join her in laughing too. "Well, I do have one."

"This is what people dating celebrities have to experience, right?"

"Right..."

"Not that we're dating." Taylor seems to have realized what she said. "I just mean that it's fascinating that this stuff actually happens. Next, you'll be asking me to sign an NDA."

"Wow, how did you know that it just came back from the notary?" I tease.

Taylor laughs.

"Well, thank you for the head's up. Can you send me the actual video so I know what to expect?"

"Sure," I say and send her the link.

"Thanks, I'll watch it later. I should get going, I need to get back to painting. I'm almost done with the portrait of you," she says and I can practically hear the smile in her voice.

"Wow," is all I can think of to say.

"Talk soon," she says and hangs up before I can ask anything else.

Two hours later, when I'm at work, Taylor finally responds.

> well at least I look cute in the video, I chose the right colour dress

> you always look cute

I hit send, the response coming out naturally, and then I experience several moments of agony when I read it back. *Oh god, what have I done?* I glance up, making sure that there's no customers waiting so I can go back to my phone.

> thank you
>
> you look pretty in the video, so I'll take cute

> you can have pretty too, there's no rule that only one of us can have each adjective

> okay, then I take dibs on gorgeous too
>
> you can have angelic for free, it suits you

> thank you for your generosity

> speaking of generous, want to come pick up your portrait tomorrow?

> I get to keep it? I'm not sure if I want to hang a picture of myself in my place, it feels a bit too self-centred

wow, you're not one of those divas who has a picture of yourself in every room? I'm almost disappointed

I laugh at the image of me being someone like that.

> just tell me what time to be there tomorrow and I'll see you then

I'm still smiling by the time we end our text convo but that doesn't last long when I see the herd of people heading towards the café for their post-work pick-me-ups. By the time I'm on my break, I finally look at all the other notifications I have that I've been ignoring. I scroll past the spam bots, the few texts from reporters and distant acquaintances who only reach out when I'm in the news, and open up the Quixotic chat.

TRAVIS

\<link\>

TRAVIS

look at what we have here. our first national headline in a year and it's about the person brodie told us was just another fellow artist

JONES

if that's just a fellow artist, I wonder how you look at your lovers

JONES

even that baseball cap can't hide how smitten you are

> omg shut up
>
> I was just playing a new song for her

I throw in the bait of the new song, knowing that tidbit should be enough to turn the conversation away from my love life and more towards our band and the next album. It's a conversation we've been needing to have for a while, so they should take the bait. RJ, the ever-loyal bestie, takes the hint.

> **RJ**
> new song?
>
> **TRAVIS**
> wow she must be special if you're sharing the first draft with her
>
> **TRAVIS**
> have I been replaced? should I be worried?
>
> don't worry, I'll send you a video edit of us soon to soothe you
>
> **TRAVIS**
> thank you, I look forward to it
>
> **RJ**
> I still can't believe no one ships brodie and me together, I swore when brodie moved to canada I expected all the fans to think we were moving in together
>
> they would think that if you weren't so into jones on stage
>
> **JONES**
> why drag me into this?

Travis and I are often the subject of shipper videos, and while we don't encourage it or fall into it, we know it happens. Though we love each other like brothers, there's definitely a corner of the internet that seems to relish imagining us together, and while I would find that kind of dynamic cute to read or watch TV about, I've never felt that way about anyone in our band. If anything, I think the fandom is sleeping on whatever it is that RJ and Jones have; but that's neither here nor there.

> **TRAVIS**
> ignore that for now, let's do a call so brodie
> can tell us about the new song

Travis calls the group again and we proceed to have another good conversation, but much shorter this time. I quickly tell them about the song, the feel of meeting someone new and wanting them to get to know you, and they congratulate me on getting my creative mojo back. I'm able to deflect any further questions about Taylor by interrogating Jones about what he's been up to, but he only provides us vague responses. By the time the call has ended, I've promised the boys to send them the song next week, after I make some tweaks. I'll have to record it in my makeshift home studio, and the thought of bringing out my recording equipment from storage fills me with a thrill. This is what I've missed about creating music.

With one last promise to try and tell them things before they make the national news, we end the call and I have to go back to work, hoping that the baseball cap I'm wearing is enough to avoid any eagle-eyed fans.

CHAPTER SEVEN

The next day, I've dressed a little fancier than usual to view the painting, trying to lean in to my excitement for once. I ring the doorbell to Taylor's studio and we go through the usual pleasantries of exchanging hellos, removing shoes, then I follow Taylor to her studio.

Repeating the first time I met her here, she does a 'ta-da' gesture as she points to the painting in the middle of the studio.

It's a portrait of me, but it doesn't look like me. Or at least, not how I see myself. The tied-up hair in the portrait looks fantastic, and I have this far-off look in my eyes. And. . . I'm smiling.

She's used a dark background, almost as if capturing me on a stage with a spotlight on me. And the warm shading of the light makes me look ethereal. It's a great piece of work, and I suddenly understand why artists have paintings of themselves commissioned.

"Wow, this is great," I say as I walk closer.

Up close, the portrait is even more unbelievable. She has captured my eye colour (hazel) perfectly, and despite this being a flat surface, I look so 3D. It's fascinating.

"Do you like it?" Taylor asks and I turn to her.

She's fidgeting with her hands and I notice for the first time that she's nervous.

"It's wild how much I like this, considering it's a painting of me," I reply honestly.

She smiles and hugs me in excitement. She pulls away before I can react.

"Oh, sorry, I got too excited."

"That's okay," I assure her.

I clear my throat and she misinterprets the gesture as me asking for space, so she takes a step back. How do I tell her it's so I wouldn't stutter from nervousness?

"If it's okay with you, can I take a picture of you next to it?" she asks.

Taylor turns and grabs a stool from the corner of the room, which she places right next to the wooden easel.

"Sure, but only if you tie my hair like last time. It'll match the portrait aesthetics better."

"Of course," Taylor says, moving to stand behind me as I sit on the stool.

When I'm sitting down, she's exactly my height.

She fixes my hair and steps in front of me.

"Now for the front," she says and begins fixing the front part of my hair that is perpetually unruly.

She smooths down the right side and the left, finally searching my face for the overall look.

I can't take my eyes off her, and when she finally makes eye contact again, I smile.

She smiles back and I blurt out the only thing I can think of, "Can I kiss you?"

If she's surprised, she doesn't show it. She steps closer and answers the question with a slight nod, before kissing me first.

Her left arm curls around me, pulling us closer, and I relish every second of it. When she takes a step back to break up the kiss, I know I must look ridiculous with my large smile and full-body blush.

"How am I supposed to take a picture now?" She laughs, stepping closer to wrap me in a hug.

"It'll go away soon, I think." I laugh too.

"You're probably the only person I know who blushes this easily. How do you do live concerts in that state?"

"To be fair, I usually can't see the audience and I'm sure none of them would be as pretty as you."

Taylor leans back to stare at me. "You're such a sweet talker, has anyone told you that?"

"Nope, probably because I don't usually speak to anyone."

She shakes her head and takes a step away from our embrace, fixing my hair again but from a greater distance.

"Okay, let's get this picture done."

After a series of pictures in which I'm sure my smile probably looks too gleeful, considering the aesthetic masterpiece that is displayed next to me, Taylor puts her phone down and grabs my hand to tug me off the stool.

"Follow me," she says as she leads me towards the stairs that are at the front of the studio, and up.

At the top of the stairs is a large bedroom, full of even more art that frames a queen-sized bed. She guides me to sit down at the edge of the bed, straddling me as she sits on my lap.

"Oh," is the only thing I can think of to say.

I want to look around the room, explore the many pieces of art, but I am admittedly very distracted by the sight in front of me.

"I know, I got lucky, right? It's so hard to find good lofts these days," she says, glancing around the room.

"R-right," I respond.

"So, should we continue what you started earlier?"

I nod and Taylor kisses me again, taking charge.

I am putty in her hands.

I'm breathless, floating as she moves closer to me. I want to touch her, feel her against me, but I'm afraid that if I do, I'll come down to earth and away from the heaven I find myself in.

She moves away from me after what feels like a long time but must've been only a few minutes.

"So, let's do this again sometime?" she asks as she stands up. She straightens her shirt from where I must've clenched it.

It takes a few seconds for me to string together a coherent sentence and I can only agree.

She leans down and gives me a quick peck on the lips. "Good."

The smile on my face must be far too ridiculous because she smiles and shakes her head, walking back down the stairs.

"I have some more painting to do, I'll text you later," she waves as she walks away.

Oh my god, what just happened?

I know I'm humming a little bit more than usual at Love A Latte Books the next day, but I can't help it. The morning rush of customers are polite as ever and one yoga teacher even marvels at how positive I am for so early in the morning. When Bea arrives to take over for the lunch shift, she comments on it as we clean up the cups together.

"Received some good news lately?"

"Something like that," I respond. No point in sharing all my business, as much as I am dying to tell her.

This *thing*, if I'm permitted to think of it as that, with Taylor is too new. Too precious. I want to keep it for myself just a little bit longer.

A customer, a local author actually, interrupts our brief reprieve from work and I stand back as Bea does her schmoozing and serving.

While I make the drink, she talks to them about local events and stocking their book, and by the time they've walked away, she is in a positively chipper mood. Her brainstorming about the possible events and collaborations distracts her from my own good mood and I listen attentively as she starts to list all her ideas.

I'm content for Bea to keep blabbering on for the rest of my shift, but another customer interrupts us.

"Matcha iced latte, please," Taylor says, smiling right at me.

I return her smile with one of my own, while Bea rings up the order.

"Whatcha doing here?" I attempt to appear nonchalant.

"I just felt like working from a coffee shop today. I have to start preparing for a wedding gig I have next weekend."

"Oh, that's fun," Bea interjects, glancing at me.

"Definitely," Taylor responds.

While I make the drink, I can hear Bea interrogate Taylor. She starts by asking her about her work, what she's been up to, and about my singing, clearly referencing the video that has now hit every single music and tabloid publication known to man, much to my horror. We tend to get decent press once in a blue moon, and it's usually about the latest thing Travis is up to, now that he's a bona fide Hollywood actor. Anything to do with me usually only makes it onto our fan blogs and the occasional *TMZ* update, but considering that the original video got over 12 million views and an article in *Entertainment Weekly*, it's snowballed beyond our normal fan base.

"There's nothing to share about it." I interrupt the conversation, bringing Taylor's drink over to the end of the counter where she waits.

"I'm just saying, we've all read the articles. I just want to be one of the first to hear any new music, is all." Bea tries to defend herself.

"If you say so." I roll my eyes as Taylor snickers at our banter.

"Come join me when you're done with your shift?" Taylor asks, nodding towards the empty tables in the sci-fi section.

I nod and she walks off. Bea doesn't miss a moment, elbowing me when she joins me at the pick-up side of the counter.

"What's the story there?"

"What story?" I aim for casual, but my cheeks warm of their own violation and I'm grateful for the face mask I decided to wear today in an effort to add an extra layer of anonymity, as the baseball caps are starting to get more recognizable.

"Are you blushing?" Bea asks, moving closer to study my face.

"What? N-no," I say, taking a step back.

A new voice chimes in. "And what's going on here?"

As if it's part of a sitcom I didn't know I was in, Steph, Bea's girlfriend, has arrived.

Bea steps away from me and runs around the counter, forgetting the fact that she's at work. One slightly inappropriate kiss later, Steph turns back to me.

"I couldn't steal your girl even if I tried," I say. "Bea was just asking me a personal question."

Steph rolls her eyes and squeezes Bea.

"Babe, we talked about this. Not everyone is living out their romcom, just because you are."

"No, but they could be. I see the way Brodie's eyes twinkle when a certain someone walks in."

Bea looks towards the area of the store where Taylor is working, and Steph's eyes follow the movement.

"Oh, the painter? She's pretty." Steph nods her approval, as if it's needed. Her comment is rewarded with a swat to the arm from Bea.

"Not for me," Steph clarifies. "For Brodie."

"You both are ridiculous. Please save the PDA for later because I'm about to end my shift and Bea has a job to do."

Bea steps away from Steph, extremely reluctantly it seems, and goes back to the counter.

"Excuse me for wanting to celebrate our anniversary."

"That's what the evening is for," I say, shrugging off my apron and folding it underneath the counter to be cleaned later.

"I know," Bea responds, punctuating the statement with a wink.

"Gross." I bump Bea with my hip on my way out, and leave her to continue to make eye hearts at her girlfriend.

I sit down across Taylor at the table she's working at, sketching into what I now recognize as her go-to sketchbook, while she looks at something on her iPad for reference.

"Sorry, am I interrupting?" I ask as she glances up at me.

"No, not at all." She puts the pencil down and looks towards me. "So, I got you something."

"What?" I ask, surprised.

"It's nothing much, here," Taylor says, taking a small gift bag out of her backpack.

I open the bag to find a baseball hat inside. It's navy blue with the words 'musical genius' in a white font on them. It's so ridiculous that I laugh as I take off my black baseball cap and put it on instead.

"It looks wonderful on you," Taylor says, looking pleased with herself.

"Thank you, but I feel like, if the point of this gift was to remain low-key, it's kind of failing on that front."

"Well, at least if someone recognizes you, it'll make for a fun story. I saw it and thought of you. And it's a thank you in advance gift, because I'm going to post the portrait later today."

"You don't need to thank me for it, you did a great job on the painting. I still can't believe you see me that way."

"What way am I supposed to see you?"

I let the question linger in my brain for a little bit.

"I'm not quite sure," I say.

This would probably be the time to hit on her, tell her that I want her to see me as someone worthy of her time and attention, but the painting is not about that. It's about me, all of me, flaws and all. And the painting she made is almost too perfect.

"Well, let me know when you figure it out." As with everything I say, Taylor seems to accept it with no issue.

I'm content to sit in silence for a bit longer, watching as she flips through her phone. When she's done, Taylor hands me her phone, where a photo and caption are waiting to be posted.

"Here, is this okay to post?"

The photo is of me sitting next to the portrait, with my hair tied up and the dreamy look on my face that I tend to get around her. The resemblance between the portrait and me is uncanny. How did she manage to capture this side of myself, before even I recognized it?

The caption is warm, reading: 'Thank you @brodiequixotic for your trust with this portrait. Excited to add this to my repertoire.'

I hand the phone back to Taylor, noticing that her usual smile has faltered a little bit. Is she nervous, perhaps?

"The post is fine, thanks for asking me first."

"Phew!" She exhales and shakes out her hands.

It's the first time I've seen her be so nervous, and it's somewhat comforting to know that even someone as talented as her can get scared sometimes.

"I'm doing it," she says, more to herself than me.

I smile as she goes back to her phone.

"Okay, done!" she says as she hits 'post,' throwing her phone down.

"Yay!" I quietly tap my hands together in a clap.

We are in a café, after all.

"I know that social media and putting yourself out there are so important to making it as an artist these days but it's probably the hardest thing for me to do. I feel like I'm too exposed when I do it."

"I feel the same way, much to my company's chagrin."

"Don't you own your company?" Taylor asks.

"Well, we all own a part of it; we're like four co-owners and then our longtime PR person Seoyun handles all the actual business stuff. So, I guess it's to the chagrin of everyone except me. The guys are so good at putting themselves out there and engaging with fans, but I'm not that way at all."

"Really? I feel like you've been posting a bit more lately."

"Well, it's easy to post pictures of random things I like, like the taste of a good new coffee, the changing colour of the trees at the park..." I trail off, not wanting to go on too long.

"And my art?" Taylor teases.

"Of course. If you didn't quite figure it out, I'm obsessed with it."

And *you*, I'm tempted to say. But I don't.

"Well, thank you." Taylor smiles and picks up her pencil again. "Sorry, I'd love to keep talking but I need to at least finish these first sketches today. Let's hang out sometime soon?"

Agreeing to plan something later, I head out, after wishing Taylor well with her work. Normally, I'd offer to keep her company but I'm inspired by Taylor's hard work so I head home and pick up my notebook again. I guess there's no time like the present to refine this song.

Two weeks later, in between working at the café and going on creative dates with Taylor, I have a complete song and a draft to present to Travis. On a video call from my desk where I've created my makeshift studio, we work on the song until we both feel like it's good enough to share with our sound engineers. It's scary, but somehow I feel good about it.

"You should do a showcase, a small show or something, to get hype for it before you release the song officially."

"I don't know if I could do a whole show by myself. What would I even do to keep people entertained?"

"Well, you can sing acoustic versions of our hit songs. A cover or two. You did always want to cover a few songs beyond just posting them to YouTube."

The idea isn't bad, and I mull it over.

"Okay, let me ask Seoyun what she thinks, the next time I talk to her."

"Good idea. You can always ask some of the other guys if they'd want to come and help with a song or two. I would come and join you, but you know my shoot schedule has me here for another few months."

"How's that going, by the way? I still can't believe you're going to be on a Netflix show."

"I know." Travis laughs. "It's wild. Speaking of, I have to go to read over some lines. Text me updates, okay?"

I agree and we end the call. I always feel inspired after talking to him, and with his confidence about my work seeping into me, I call Seoyun before I can chicken out.

Another hour flies by as we brainstorm and catch up, and now that she's involved, somehow this whole thing doesn't seem as scary. Yes, I'll probably be more nervous than humanly possible when it goes public, but if I want my career to keep moving anywhere, I guess it's time to put myself out there.

Maybe in more than one way.

CHAPTER EIGHT

It's taken me a week to build up the mental fortitude, but eventually, I manage to get all the guys on a group call. As I stare at their faces through my laptop screen, a nervous energy fills me. It's so weird actually seeing them, as we usually talk on the phone, and they must be thinking the same thing because Travis interrupts the awkward silence with his usual good-natured chuckle.

"This is weird. Brodie, is this an intervention?" he asks.

"Yeah, what's with the cryptic message?" Jones chimes in.

RJ nods from where I can see him on his screen, the background looking similar to Jones's.

"It's not an intervention," I begin, "more like an announcement."

Travis immediately claps his hands.

"I knew it, you're going to release your new song soon."

RJ and Jones immediately burst into their own whoops of excitement and I have to gesture for them to calm down.

"Relax, relax. It's not that. I mean, that's next. But first, I have to tell you something. No interruptions, please."

They all nod and Jones even puts on his glasses, in what I recognize as a gesture to signal he's really listening. It makes me smile and I remind myself that, no matter what happens, these guys are my brothers.

"Well, you know how I've been here for a while 'figuring my shit out'? I think I've figured it out." I pause and the boys smile at me, so I continue. "I'm non-binary and I use they/them pronouns. My friends here know and I've told Seoyun to avoid gendering me in some future communications, but I figured I should tell y'all first."

"Oh, that's great, man!" Jones says before slapping himself. "Not *man,* man. You know... sibling?"

The rest of us burst into laughter at that.

"It's okay, I know it'll take some getting used to. I hope y'all don't take offence at the fact that I didn't tell you sooner... It's just that I don't think I could handle a rejection from my best friends if y'all didn't approve."

"First off, you don't need our approval," Travis jumps in, "and we would never reject a fellow artist for being themselves. That's ridiculous."

"Yeah, bud," RJ says, "I'm almost offended that you thought we'd actually be mad."

I roll my eyes at them and they seem to take it as the loving sibling gesture it is, because they're all smiling when I look back at the screen.

"I wish we were there in person so we could hug," Jones says, his face turning into the puppy dog look that gets the fans riled up.

"Well, what are you doing in three weeks?"

"Nothing..." RJ says, eyeing me suspiciously.

"Then you can come see me at my solo showcase," I tell them with a pompous air.

The screaming and hooting are more intense than the first time, and I swear some of it echoes from RJ's computer.

It takes another hour for us to get through all the details of RJ's visit and random questions that pop up from the others, but at the end of the call, I'm feeling more relieved. I text the first person I can think of to plan a celebratory round of drinks.

∽

"Are flowers too much?" I ask as I hand them to Taylor.

"No, they're perfect. Come in," she says and opens the door wider for me.

While I would've preferred to take her out, I know my solo showcase announcement is set to be released tomorrow and I don't want to risk the media lumping in a story about my personal life with it, if the restaurant happens to have someone who recognizes me.

Taylor is wearing a dress, a simple white mid-length one, and it sways nicely as she walks away to her kitchen. She finds a vase and is putting the flowers in them when I step into the kitchen, nervously smoothing my hands along my jeans. I place the wine bottle I brought onto the island.

"So, what's the occasion?" she asks.

"Well, I'm going to be busy for the next little bit, so I wanted to make sure to see you before then. I have a showcase to plan and all that."

"Showcase? Can I get tickets?"

"Better, you can be there backstage," I tell her, stepping around the island to move closer to her.

She steps closer to me, wrapping her arms around the small of my back to look up at me.

"Oh, backstage. . ." she says thoughtfully, smiling. "I don't think I've ever been backstage before."

"You'd better get used to it. Dating me and all."

I hope the blush on my cheeks doesn't show. It's probably the most impressive line I've said to a girl I like and I almost want to get out my notebook to write it down, but Taylor surprises me with a kiss and my normal overthinking shuts down.

"That would be nice," she says when we break apart.

She pats my back and steps away.

"Sorry, I didn't invite you here to maul your mouth. You promised some drinks?"

She grabs wine glasses from a cupboard and a corkscrew from a drawer. I uncork the wine bottle successfully, which surprises me more than her because I have never been so smooth in my entire life.

"Sorry, there's no couch so we have to go drink this upstairs," she says and I follow her to her bedroom, with my glass in one hand and the bottle in the other.

Sitting on her bed drinking wine should be weird, but it isn't. I tell her all about my upcoming showcase, how the boys responded so well to my gender reveal (which is a weird way to phrase it, and we laugh about that too), and she tells me about her latest work.

The bottle is halfway gone when I hold my hand out to her, first putting my wine glass down on the floor. She joins me in putting down her glass so I can grab her hand.

"I know I'm in no place to ask anyone to make a commitment to me and it's too early for that," I start, "but I just wanted to let you know that you're the only person I do this with."

"Drink wine in their bed?" She has a mischievous look in her eye and I smile as I shake my head.

"Talk about my feelings. Kiss. Share my songs before they're even ready. Be myself."

"I can't join you in sharing songs, because I don't write them, but I feel the same."

It doesn't take long for the wine bottle to be forgotten as we lazily kiss, clearly competing to create the best make-out session. Though I've already written a song for her, I leave her place knowing that I'll soon be writing many more.

CHAPTER NINE

The weeks fly by and I am now sweating my ass off in nervousness backstage at the Danforth Music Hall.

"You'll be fine, you've got this." RJ claps me on the shoulder, repeating a familiar gesture that he's done on every tour we've done together.

I take a deep breath, trying to focus on the comfort of that moment.

It's fine, Brodie. You've got this.

The door opens and I'm surprised to see Taylor walking in with Jones.

"Jones!" I exclaim, barreling into him with a hug.

He takes the hug in stride, matching my enthusiasm.

"I had to come support my buddies," Jones says, pulling away from me and hugging RJ.

While they communicate silently in the stares that only they can decipher, I reach out for Taylor and grab her by the hand.

"Thank you for being here," I say, meaning every word.

"I wouldn't dare miss it. When else would I get to see Brodie Bailey, of the famous Quixotic, perform for such a small intimate audience?"

"1500 people is hardly a small audience," I say.

"So, who's this?" RJ asks, pointedly looking at the way I have Taylor's hand gripped in mine.

"As if you're one to talk, what's with this?" I use my free hand to point between RJ and Jones.

Jones has his arm around RJ's waist, keeping them standing close together. It looks oddly intimate for the two of them and being around enough openly queer couples now, compared to the straight energy we'd see backstage at every show, it has me side eyeing their interactions.

RJ seems to realize it too because he steps away and nervously chuckles.

"Don't think you can get out of this." He turns his attention to Taylor instead and she falls for it.

"Hi, I'm Taylor. Brodie and I are friends." She holds out her hand for RJ to shake and he does so while snickering, as does Jones.

"Friends," Jones says. "Brodie doesn't have a lot of those. Especially not ones that they hold hands with."

"Shut up," I say, whacking him on the arm.

I blush at how happy the conversation makes me, from hearing my new pronouns to their brotherly teasing.

A knock at the door interrupts whatever else Jones is about to say and Charlie, the show producer, pops their head in.

"Two minutes to showtime, Brodie."

I nod and shake out my hands again. I reach for my guitar and pluck on it nervously.

Jones squeezes my shoulders. "You've got this. And if anyone asks, I'm not here."

"You brat. Stop making this about yourself when it's about to be my show," I say.

"Good luck, Brodie. I'll watch with Jones at the side stage," Taylor tells me. She surprises me by giving me a peck on the lips.

"For courage," she says, smiling wide when I start blushing.

Charlie interrupts RJ and Jones's hooting and hollering and I follow them to the stage, laughing while trying to escape their teasing.

At the side of the stage, I take a deep breath.

The cheers from the crowd shock me when I step out. The venue is full, and I see even the people at the top of the balcony waving and cheering to me.

"Wow, hello everyone," I say into the mic at the centre of the stage and the cheering resumes.

I move through my setlist with ease, thanking the past version of me for practising so much. A cover of Laufey's "Bewitched" captivates the crowd and my new song, played live for the first time, is met with a warm cheer. It's weird singing so raw and exposed, especially as the crowd can't sing along, but by the reaction, I think the single will be well received when it's on streaming platforms next week.

When I end the show after a few more songs, I put down my guitar and walk around the edge of the stage, waving to the fans. A fan holds up a poster of the portrait that Taylor painted of me and a gold sharpie.

"Please sign this for me!" they yell.

I comply and I'm impressed by how wild this is. When Seoyun suggested that we collaborate with Taylor to have this portrait made as merch, I thought it was weird. Me appear as artwork on someone's wall? But if it was a chance for Taylor to get more exposure and for some extra income ahead of the slow wedding season (people in Canada do *not* like to get married in the winter), then I had to do it.

I sign a few more posters and wave a bit more, running off the stage.

"You were so wonderful!" Taylor is shouting into my ear as she wraps me in a hug.

The crew behind her is cheering for me and RJ and Jones are next to hug me. Taylor takes the microphone out of my hand and steps aside.

"You were phenomenal. You need to release a solo album yesterday," Jones tells me.

I laugh it off and pull him in for a hug. A staff member taps me on the shoulder, looking apologetic about interrupting. They're holding the merch T-shirt for me to change into and I quickly pull it on, the need to hurry overtaking my need to feel shy around everyone else. When I'm done, Taylor hands me back the microphone.

"Ready for the encore?" I ask, now turning to RJ.

"You know it." RJ nods and gestures to the microphone he has in his hand.

We've agreed to let me go on stage first for the encore, to introduce him, and then we'll sing one of our more popular songs. I didn't sing it earlier and I could definitely hear a few grumbles from the crowd about it.

When the crowd's "Encore, encore!" cheers start to fade out, I run back onto the stage.

"You didn't think I'd end the show without singing 'Someday', did you?"

The crowd cheers, louder than they did for my new song. I can't even blame them.

Picking up my guitar, I move to sit down on the stool that's been placed in front of the mic by stage staff.

"I'm feeling a bit tired tonight. Should I call a friend to help me with this one?"

I pretend to wipe sweat off my forehead as the crowd cheers, even louder this time.

"Hey, bud, heard you needed some help?" RJ's melodic voice comes through the speakers and the crowd roars.

It takes him a few seconds to actually walk out on stage and he's wearing a T-shirt that says, "I <3 Brodie."

I swear he wasn't wearing it a minute ago, and I laugh as I spot it.

"You may know this guy from a little band called Quixotic. Give it up for Raj, or as you know him, RJ!"

The crowd roars this time as he comes to stand next to me.

"If you know this one, sing along," I say into the mic as RJ and I are off.

When the song ends, there may or may not be some tears in my eyes. Seeing the crowd hugging their loved ones, holding up their phone flashlights and swaying side to side has me all sorts of emotional. I wouldn't be here without the support of these people and my friends, including RJ, and the moment just gets to me.

The show ends properly after another song and a heartfelt speech.

"I promise to become a better artist, and see you all again soon," I say to the audience as they clap for the final time.

RJ and I bow, and run off to the backstage area.

Jones pulls me in for a hug and a sincere, "I love you," and I return the sentiment.

After thanking all the crew and stage producers, I make it to the dressing room, where my nondescript change of clothes is waiting for me, and so is Taylor. She's sitting on the couch, scrolling through her phone.

"Wow, you really did cry during 'Someday,'" she says, smiling up at me when I flop onto the couch next to her.

I groan. "Ugh, is that already up everywhere?"

"Yes, it's all over social media."

"Great." I sigh and wrap an arm around her.

I pull her closer to me and she smiles as she puts her phone down.

"Where are RJ and Jones?" she asks.

"They left already. Jones had the taxi ready for right when the show ended," I tell her.

"They seemed awfully close. I mean, I know they're bandmates but they did seem closer than that."

"Yeah, they've been that way for a while now. I need to ask him about it but haven't had the time. . ." I trail off, as I have something more important to talk to her about. "So, what are you doing for the rest of the night?"

Being on stage has left me with a confidence that I normally don't possess, but if I was able to conquer this stage, there must be some other things I can do now. I am a bit unstoppable now, aren't I?

"I have no plans, why?"

"What about tomorrow?"

Taylor must catch the mischievous tone that I was going for because she leans in closer to me, reaching up towards my cheek.

"Day off, why?"

I lean down so we're only an inch apart.

"Afterparty at my place?" I whisper.

She nods and I kiss her, trying to pour the feeling of all those sleepless nights I spent thinking of her. Of the way she is so supportive of me and my career. How amazingly talented she is.

A knock at the door interrupts us and I take a moment to straighten out my shirt from where she gripped it.

"Sorry, boss." Charlie pokes their head in again. "Just wanted to give you a head's up that we have the car ready out front. Security is ready to escort you out."

"Sure, thanks," I nod and stand, reaching out for Taylor with my hand.

She shakes her head, reaching for my guitar and putting it in my hands instead.

"Don't want to end up on *TMZ* tomorrow," she says, sounding apologetic.

"Totally get it," I say, and I do.

Not everyone is cut out for this whirlwind.

"Do you want to borrow my hat?" Charlie asks, whipping the 'quixotic 4ever' hat off their head. "Not that I meant to overhear but I get it. Besides, giving my hat away to someone Brodie cares about would be an honour."

"Are you sure?" I ask.

"Totally." Charlie places the hat in a speechless Taylor's hands and she finally smiles as she stares at the font on the hat.

"Here, we'll match," I tell her as I put on the baseball hat she gifted me.

She smiles and ties up her hair, hiding it beneath the hat.

Taylor heads out towards the car first, keeping her head down while I wait for security's clear to follow her.

After she's in, I jog out of the venue and keep my eyes down, making sure to follow the venue's security staff, who are waiting to make sure no fan crosses any boundaries. While I hear a few scattered cheers as folks seem to realize what's going on, by the time I make it into the taxi, all is fine.

The taxi takes off and I tell them my building's address as we leave the cheers behind.

"Wow, why are people so loud these days? Must be some big show," the taxi driver comments and all we can do is laugh.

I'm sweating a little as I unlock my door, nervous that Taylor will learn more about me and somehow realize that actually she hates me.

I try to dismiss the intrusive thought, remembering that, if she actually she hated me, she wouldn't be here (thank you, therapy).

I stand near the front entrance as she walks around and looks over my bookshelf, my little recording desk in the corner, and the various postcards that line my walls. It's not unlike the curious looks I've taken around her studio and it strikes me as an artistic move; wanting to see how a person's place looks as a way to get to know them.

She sits down on the couch and pats the cushion next to her, the one closest to the door.

"Come, sit," she says.

"Well, what do you think?"

She looks around again before turning back to me.

"It's very you," she says, smiling.

I laugh nervously. "What does that mean? Do I need to suddenly rearrange everything? Are the postcards of cities where I've been on tours too embarrassing?"

"No, I like it all. If I got to go to this many places, I'd have it all displayed too. Why not?"

"Right..."

I'm nervous. Why am I so nervous?

"What did you think of the show?" I ask, trying to find a topic of conversation.

"I already told you that you were amazing," she says, scooting closer to me.

I feel myself flush and I know the bright overhead lights of the living room must reveal it so well to her.

"Well... I mean, I wouldn't mind hearing you say that again."

"Oh," Taylor says, moving closer. She leans forward so she can study my face more closely. "You were very good, Brodie," she whispers, searching my eyes as she says it.

Whatever she was aiming for seems to have worked because I feel myself blush deeper.

"You have a praise kink, don't you?" she asks, moving away from me.

Somehow, though I did not think it was remotely possible, I find myself blushing even harder.

"I guess I am that easy to read," I say, wiping the nervous sweat from the back of my neck.

Taylor smiles and reaches out for my arm, forcing me to let go of my neck. She grabs my now-free hand and stands up.

"Why don't you show me your bedroom?"

Speechless, all I can do is nod as she leads me through the open door off the living room.

Thank God I straightened my bedsheets earlier. I think I'd die of embarrassment if I'd somehow left the room in disarray.

Taylor pushes me onto the bed and I stare at the ceiling for a few seconds before I feel her crawl over me, and her face soon appears above mine.

"Is this okay?" she asks, sounding unsure.

"More than okay," I say as I shift so I can lean up and towards her mouth.

"Good," she confirms as she meets me halfway, kissing me back.

If I thought I was in heaven with her previously, then now I must've ascended to a new planet. Kissing slowly, exploring each other. I've dreamed about this moment after our first kiss a few weeks ago and now that it's here, I can confirm that it was worth the wait.

Taylor breaks away after a moment, looking down at me. She shifts so she's straddling me and she tugs me upwards so we're chest to chest.

"Take this off," she says, tugging the bottom of my shirt.

"You too," I say and she doesn't hesitate to copy my frantic action.

Anything else I was going to say is lost on my lips as I take in her lacy bra.

"You like?" she asks mischievously.

I can only nod.

"What am I going to do with you?" she says, as if to herself.

I should respond, say something intelligent or smart, but having her so close to me makes me lose all reason. It takes me a few seconds longer to respond than I'd like but I smartly say, "Whatever you'd like. Please."

Taylor removes her bra and wraps her arms around me, pulling me in for another kiss.

"You're going to be good, aren't you?"

A whimper is all I can respond with.

She bites my lip and that whimper is replaced by a moan. She continues her small bites and occasionally adds some kisses as she works her way down my body. When she reaches my pants, she helps me tug them off and she does the same for hers, forcing us off the bed.

It's the first time I've been naked in front of someone in a while and I should feel embarrassed, as I did all those times before. I should feel nervous at someone looking at me and perceiving me, but I'm not. Taylor has already seen who I am inside, more than most, and it is this comfort that stops me spiralling out of nervousness.

She chose to be here, and this thought makes me more determined to show her how much I care for her.

"You're beautiful," I say as we stand in front of each other and I move my eyes over all of her.

"You too," she says, stepping towards me.

"One second," I say, stepping back. "Let me just take it all in."

She rolls her eyes but does a little spin.

"Happy?"

"Almost. Why don't you lie back down and let me taste you like I've been dreaming of for the past few weeks?"

"If you insist." She follows my instructions.

While the focus of this exercise was all about her, I enjoy her notes of encouragement and tugs on my hair way too much for me to think this was a selfless action.

I almost lose myself when she calls me a "good girl"; the moment strikes me as both sexy and intimate and I know it'll haunt me in my dreams later. She asked me about the endearment and feminine forms of address a few weeks ago on one of our creative dates, and I almost fall more in love with her for remembering what I've told her.

I'm left speechless and out of breath by the time we finish sufficiently exploring each other, and I take immense pleasure in being the little spoon in our post-coital cuddle.

"So, should we go on proper dates next?" I ask as Taylor strokes my hair from where it fans out beneath me.

"Sure, we can do a movie and dinner at my place. Sex for dessert."

I laugh but can't say I disagree. "Sounds like the perfect plan."

The next day, I wake up with the most beautiful woman in my arms and I almost scare myself with the thought of how badly I wish I could wake up this way every day.

"Good morning, famous singer," Taylor teases as she opens her eyes.

"Good morning, talented painter." I smile as she rolls her eyes.

"What's for breakfast?"

"I can order in," I say, yawning and standing up.

Taylor whistles as I walk away and I wiggle my ass a little extra for her.

It takes me a few moments to find my phone from where I left it at the front entrance yesterday and I immediately regret grabbing it first thing in the morning, as I'm greeted with way too many notifications.

Not wanting to deal with this naked, I run back to my bedroom and grab a pair of sweatpants from my dresser before sitting at the foot of the bed.

"Sorry, I need to go through this first," I say to Taylor, who's still in bed, and she nods in understanding.

She stands to use the washroom and I'm rewarded with the sight of her in one of my favourite T-shirts when she comes back out.

She sits next to me and reaches for my hand.

"It's okay if you need to work today, I'm sure you must have a lot to do."

Having read through most of it by now, it's not that bad as I thought.

"No, I'll take the day off. I can respond to all these media requests later. For now, I just need to post something about the show."

"Do you know what you'll say?"

"Yeah. I think I do." I put my phone down and grab her other hand in mine.

"You're not going to run away if things get even more ridiculous from here, are you?"

I have to ask the question, even if the answer will hurt.

Taylor shakes her head. "Sorry, you're stuck with me now."

"Good."

I kiss her and she has to interrupt our make-out session a few minutes later with a, "Don't you have work to do?"

I groan as I pull away and grab my phone instead.

"I hate being an adult," I whine.

"There, there. I'll order breakfast for us then. What's your address?"

I give her my address and buzzer code and tell her to put it on my credit card, which I give to her after finding my wallet in the corner of my room from where it had flung out of my pants in our make-out session yesterday.

I save a few pictures that Seoyun received from the professional photographers last night, a selfie that RJ and I took, and a photo from the side stage that Jones seems to have taken from his vantage point.

I respond to the rest of the band's well wishes in our group chat before opening up Instagram.

It takes me a few minutes to get the wording quite right but then I hit post before I have the nerves to chicken out. Thankfully, my notifications are already a mess from all the fans tagging me in posts last night, so I don't even have the capacity to see any replies if they pour in.

Thank you so much Toronto for welcoming me with open arms and letting your home become mine. It's been a wild few years, and while I know some have worried that I'll be leaving music, I love it too much to give up on it entirely. Thank you for your support and for cheering on my new music. Updates to come.

Thank you RJ for coming out here to support me. Thank you Jones and Travis for supporting me in all that I do. Quixotic 4ever indeed.

Thank you T for everything.

And lastly, please refer to me using they/them pronouns in any news reporting or posts related to my work, past, present or future. Please email my team for any questions.

Haters will be ignored & comments are off. Much love, Brodie <3

"There, I did it," I say aloud as I read over the post now that it's up.

I send a link of the post to the Quixotic group chat and the boys all share their love with me immediately.

I see more texts come in, this time from my friends, but I put my phone on do-not-disturb mode and leave it on my nightstand to charge. I head back to the living room where Taylor is on her phone, tears in her eyes.

"Are you okay??" I ask, alarmed.

I sit down next to her and she turns to me, pulling me in for a hug.

"I'm so proud of you," she says and I melt into her arms.

"I'm kind of proud of me too," I say, tears now emerging in my own eyes.

She strokes my hair as I release all the emotions I've kept bottled inside for who knows how long. The future and my career may be unknown for now, but at least I have the support of my friends and loved ones. And for this foolishly romantic singer, that is more than enough.

EPILOGUE

"A kiss for good luck." Taylor leans up to kiss me on the cheek.

"More," I whine as she pulls away from me.

She rolls her eyes but complies with my request and kisses my lips this time.

Whistles break us up and I playfully turn Taylor around so she's hiding behind me as my friends all cheer us on.

"Rude! That was an intimate moment." I stick my tongue out at them.

"You're the one with a show in twenty minutes." Bea shakes her head at me.

Taylor laughs and ducks back out from behind me, grabbing my hand.

"Well, thank you all for being here. I know that's Brodie's way of saying thank you," Taylor says for me.

"Of course, we wouldn't be here for anyone else," Travis says, a proud look in his eyes.

The rest of the crowd in this tiny dressing room seems to share the same look. Jenna, Bea, Travis, RJ, and Jones. And of course, the girlfriends that couldn't resist an opportunity to see a Quixotic reunion, even if it is only backstage: Gabriella and Steph. And my own girlfriend.

Taylor squeezes my hand and I squeeze it back.

"Cheers to Brodie's new album, 'New Beginnings,'" Jones yells, eliciting cheers from the rest of the group.

"Thank you all for being here for me," I say, looking around the room and trying not to get too choked up. "I would be half the person I am now, if not for all of you. Thank you for never giving up on me."

This last part is directed more to my bandmates than my friends, but I still had to say it.

RJ tackles me in a hug, and it doesn't take long for the rest of the group to join in.

Whatever happens next, whether my album flops or I have to find a new career, I am grateful for this group of people, who accepted me along the way. This is just the beginning of the next phase of my life, and I can't wait to discover how it goes.

We may have named the band after a word that means idealistic or romantic; an almost impossible hope, but standing in front of all of these people, it reminds me that it's not impossible to be yourself around the people who love you. You just have to find them, and I'm glad to have found them in this weird, big city.

"What are you thinking about in there?" Taylor asks as the hug ends and I'm left staring at all my friends.

I guess I was always quite easy to read.

"Just about how lucky I am," I say honestly.

Everyone shakes their heads at what they assume is self-deprecation but Taylor gives me a knowing smile.

"We're all pretty lucky to know you too," she says.

And with the support of my friends, I go on to play one of my best shows, knowing that this is only the beginning for Brodie Bailey.

THE END

BONUS MATERIAL

Want to read more by this author? Sign up for their newsletter at www.rochellewolf.com to get the latest on future releases and to be a part of their early reader team!

Join Rochelle Wolf's Cozy Corner on Patreon for exclusive sneak peeks on the author's upcoming releases and bonus chapters. A bonus chapter for *Room for Two* is available now, and more are on the way!

ACKNOWLEDGMENTS

Thank you so much for reading, and I hope you enjoyed this novella collection! It is no exaggeration when writers say that they could not do this without you and that is true for me. Whether you're a returning reader or a new fan, I am so thankful for the chance that you took on me and my writing. I hope you stick around for the next few books.

Thank you to the team that helped me get this done. Thank you to my sisters for being the best siblings a person could ask for. Thank you to my friends: Ambur, Joey, Jesse, Octavia, Maria, and Patty for all your support and encouragement.

Thank you Lawrie for always cheering me on and for supporting my writing, both with beta reading and editing. Thank you Annie for all your great editing on this series. Thank you to all the writers in the Beaver Tales group chat for your support & for answering any publishing questions I had. Thank you Mia for your original stunning novella covers, and Maria for creating this gorgeous bind-up cover for me.

To the beta readers who helped me along the way, with any of my novellas, I would not be here without you: Ashley M. Christiansen, Mary EmmaLee, Liv Kocinski, Avery Bridge, Lawrie from The Cat's Clause, Kimberley, Hannah of HV Editorial, Abi Walker, Karyn Defoe, Shubhr, A.A. Fairview, Dorita McPherson, Christina Franklin.

Thank you to my Patreon members for reminding me that there are readers out there who like my books. Your support means more than you know.

ABOUT THE AUTHOR

Rochelle Wolf is a Toronto-based queer writer, interested in warm love stories and books that feel like a hug. They have perfected the art of making their special interest (books) their entire career. Formerly a librarian, they now run their own book editing business. When they're not reading or writing, they enjoy watching reality TV shows and traveling. To learn more about their books, please visit their website, www.rochellewolf.com.

instagram.com/rochellewolfauthor

www.ingramcontent.com/pod-product-compliance
Lightning Source LLC
LaVergne TN
LVHW041629060526
838200LV00040B/1506